TRAIL RIDE BY THE YADKIN RIVER

Donna Winters

Bigwater Publishing LLC

www.GreatLakesRomances.com

Garden, Michigan

To girls who love horses and romance

Acknowledgments

I would like to thank the following for their contributions to this fictional endeavor:

First and foremost, my Lord and Savior, Jesus Christ, the source of my inspiration. He answers my prayers and makes all things possible!

And on the human level:

JoAnn Grote, who supplied historical facts and descriptions of North Carolina settings

Shirley and Jeannie Soest, who spent several hours sharing their knowledge of horses

Lola Sage, who took me on a long and lovely ride in her horse-drawn wagon

Shirley and Bob Slocum, who treated me to a Sunday afternoon sleigh ride on a crisp January day in 1995

Rachel Balke Heighton, who read my manuscript with unbridled enthusiasm

CONTENTS

CHAPTER 1

Tanglewood, North Carolina
July 2, 1900

The chestnut mare groaned. Sixteen-year-old Vanda Mae, still dressed in the riding breeches and shirt she'd put on the day before, roused from the bed of straw where she'd been dozing and knelt at the horse's side.

"Easy, Springer. Easy, now. I'm right here."

The mare lifted her head a trifle, snorted, and lay it down again to resume the quiet moaning she had kept up for the past several hours. In the bright afternoon light streaming through the stable window, a yellow tinge shown in the area around Springer's eye.

Vanda Mae wrapped her arms about Springer's neck and pressed her cheek against it. The smell of her mare's breath was putrid, fouling the sweet scent of the fresh straw bedding that had been brought into the stable that morning. Vanda Mae pulled away and stroked the small, diamond-shaped patch of white on Springer's face.

"I know you're mighty bad off right now, girl, but you'll get over this. You've got to!"

Springer whined.

Vanda Mae's stomach soured. How had this happened? How had the gate come open and allowed Springer out of her pasture two of days ago? Though she hadn't strayed far, she'd eaten the dirt that was blocking her innards, killing her. If only . . .

At the other end of the stable, the boot heels of Gaspar, who looked after the two dozen or so horses at Tanglewood, thudded against the floor. Moments later he entered Springer's stall. At the touch of his hand on Vanda Mae's shoulder, she turned to the short, slender man, searching his deeply tanned face as he knelt beside her and examined her horse. When he spoke, the dark eyes that met her gaze were shrouded with concern.

"*El aciete,* the oil, is not working. We must end Springer's suffering." He started to rise.

She grabbed his hand, rising with him. "Not yet, Gaspar. She just needs more time. Give her until tomorrow. *Please!"*

Taking her firmly by the wrist, he released her hold. "*Lo siento,* I am sorry, there is no other way. Even Dr. Whitehead has said so. I get my rifle." He strode off.

Tears sprang to Vanda Mae's eyes. She dropped down beside Springer, hugging her tightly. "I love you, girl!" Her throat too tight to say more, she could only think of all she'd miss with Springer gone.

Never again would the elegant mare prance across the meadow as if to say "Look at me!" when Vanda Mae was perched atop the fence watching her. Nor would the animal come galloping past Vanda Mae in "catch me if you can" playfulness when she appeared with halter and lead, only to stop a hundred feet away from her to wait patiently. And no more would Springer nuzzle her neck, nibble at her hair, and whinny in her ear as if to say, "I love you."

You've been my best friend for so many years, I don't know what I'll do without you!

Springer grunted, her complaint weak. Gaspar and the veterinarian were right. They shouldn't let the suffering continue.

The hired hand came toward her now. At the sight of his rifle, Vanda Mae bolted down the center aisle of the stable past Tassie, who was confined until the birth of her foal. Vanda Mae grabbed a halter from the tack room and ran toward the horse pasture. Hurricane and Firelight—the stallion who had sired Tassie's foal—were standing in the shade of an elm a hundred yards away.

Vanda Mae climbed onto the board fence. When she paused at the top, the crack of Gaspar's rifle shattered the stillness, sending a sharp stab deep into her. She scrambled off the fence and ran toward Hurricane, slipped the halter over his head, and climbed on.

"Go, boy!" she whispered into the animal's ear as she nudged him with her heels.

He trotted toward the gate at the far side of the meadow where she quickly dismounted and let him out onto the two-rut drive. When she mounted the grey gelding again, he seemed to read her emotions, moving from trot to canter despite the warm weather.

Though Vanda Mae's heart was at a gallop, she dared not ask Hurricane to move faster in the heat. Passing a barn, more stables, a field of corn and another of alfalfa, she followed the road into the woods that covered much of her father's four hundred acres. Two minutes later, with the clearing at the end of the drive in sight, she began to slow down. Should she turn toward the Winthrops', or toward the town of Clemmons?

Heading toward the Winthrops', the grey gelding soon cantered past the drive to their barn, then into more woods. The odor of manure grew thick in the air. Rounding a curve, Vanda Mae spotted a wagon on the road a couple hundred yards ahead traveling in the same direction. Though she didn't recognize the horses from behind, the driver with broad shoulders and red hair was Willy Jo.

"Easy, boy. Take it down. We don't want to spook Willy Jo's team." Hurricane had slowed to a trot when several pops from a shotgun sounded close by.

Hurricane bolted. Nearly coming unseated, Vanda Mae clung tight to his mane. "Whoa, Hurricane! Whoa!"

Bound on his own course, Hurricane galloped on, passing too close to Willy Jo's wagon. Behind him, hooves pounded, harnesses rattled, and Willy Jo shouted.

"Danny! Dolly! Whoa, now! Whoa!"

The team was bearing down on Vanda Mae. She pulled hard to the right. "Whoa, Hurricane! Whoa!"

Heeding her plea this time, he slowed down and moved off the road beside a cornfield.

Willy Jo's wagon barreled past, leaving a cloud of dust. Veering off the road, they made a wide circle through the corn to change directions. Taking to the road once more, they charged past Vanda Mae.

She turned and followed as they veered sharply onto the drive to their barn. But the corner was too tight.

Tipping up on two wheels, the wagon started to overturn, leaving a trail of manure behind. Willy Jo jumped free just before the buckboard crashed onto its side and separated from the team.

Still yoked together, the horses ran blind, barely missing a huge magnolia tree and the fence around a pasture. Moments later they came to a halt beside a row of tulip poplars.

Willy Jo started toward the wagon.

Vanda Mae urged Hurricane on, catching up with him before he reached it.

"Willy Jo, I'm sorry!"

He turned to her, his blue eyes flashing. "Vannie-Mae Foxe, this is a fine fix you got me in!"

"You should have had better control of your team!"

"Horsefiddles! They were okay, till you came along!"

"Hurricane spooked. I tried to get him to slow down!"

Willy Jo ran a hand through his hair. "I've a mind to *shoot* that horse!"

Vanda Mae jumped down. "Don't you ever say such a thing again!"

"He's nothing but trouble! First for your sister, now for you—*and* me. You ought to make him into a bucket of plaster and a pot of glue!" Willy Jo turned and strode off.

Heat surging up Vanda Mae's spine, she ran and shoved him, landing him smack in the spilt manure.

"Don't you *ever* threaten to shoot Hurricane again!" She wagged her finger at him.

He scrambled to his feet. Dung dropped in clumps from his overalls. His face turned the color of the clay on which Vanda Mae was standing. "You little—I'll get you for this!"

"Catch me if you can!" she taunted, starting to climb onto Hurricane.

He grabbed her by the elbow, preventing her from mounting. Somehow her feet tangled with his and she fell on her backside—right into a patch of manure.

Willy Jo offered a hand, his words as contrite as the look on his face. "Fiddles. I didn't mean for that to happen, Vannie-Mae. Truly."

Taking a fistful of the slimy manure, Vanda Mae slapped it against Willy Jo's palm, gripping tightly and pulling herself to her feet. "You're forgiven, Willy Jo. Maybe."

She released her grip and wiped her hand against the front of her breeches. Taking hold of Hurricane's halter, she turned and walked toward home. She couldn't mount him with the manure all over her behind. It would put a stain on his pale grey coat that would be almost impossible to wash off.

Her steps slowed, vividly remembering the blast of Gaspar's rifle. Her stomach soured. Tanglewood wouldn't be the same without Springer. She glanced over her shoulder. Willy Jo was inspecting his wagon, contemplating the problem of turning it upright. She went to him.

"Let me help you with that, Willy Jo."

The look he gave her sent the same message as his words. "Go home, Vannie-Mae. I don't need your kind of help. You're the one who got me into this fix."

"It's only right you let me make amends."

Willy Jo walked away from her, pausing at the rear of the wagon to inspect the axle. She followed, unwilling to be dismissed so easily.

A moment later he faced her, his nose wrinkling. "You stink."

"You stink worse."

"No point taking a bath till I get myself out of this mess."

"It will take you all afternoon to shovel that load back onto the wagon. I'll help."

"This is no job for a girl."

"I've been cleaning stables since I was old enough to fetch a manure basket. This is no different."

Willy Jo grabbed the rim of the left rear wheel and levered his weight against it. The wagon creaked but hardly budged. Moving to the front, he took the remnant of a snapped tug in his hand, then dropped the frayed leather strap in disgust. "I'll have to get new tugs from the tack room." He started in the direction of the barn. Vanda Mae followed, leading Hurricane.

A long silence ensued, a silence during which Vanda Mae pondered the mess she'd gotten Willy Jo into. Perhaps she shouldn't have stayed in the hot, steamy Piedmont to witness the birth of Tassie's first foal. Perhaps she should have gone with her mother to the cooler mountain resort of Blowing Rock where she and Rosalie had spent many summers. At least then she wouldn't have gotten Willy Jo into this stinking mess. And she wouldn't have been home to witness Springer's demise. She silently prayed that these calamities weren't an omen of things to come, that Tassie would have an easy birthing. And that it would be soon.

~~~

Willy Jo glanced at Vanda Mae. He'd seen her a time or two from a distance since he'd come home from agricultural college for the summer, but he hadn't gotten close enough to notice the changes in her till now. Her manure-stained riding breeches and oversized shirt couldn't mask the fact that she was growing into womanhood. And though he didn't want to admit it, her oval face and dark hair were a trifle prettier than her older sister, Rosalie, had been at sixteen.

He saw, too, that Vanda Mae had turned melancholy and quiet. Was she lonely, staying in the Piedmont when her good friend—his own younger brother, Bobby Dan—had gone to Blowing Rock along with both their mothers? They had almost reached the barn when he voiced his thoughts.

"You look sadder than a hog in a bathtub, Vannie-Mae. I guess you're sorry you didn't go to Blowing Rock after all."

The young girl's shoulders drooped. He touched her arm. "You're not fixing to cry, are you? Your daddy would take you there if you asked."

Vanda Mae turned away, burying her face against Hurricane's neck. A moment later, she wiped her cheek on her shirt sleeve and faced Willy Jo. "I don't care about Blowing Rock. I . . ."

"What, Vannie-Mae?"

Her face crumpled. "Springer's dead! She had colic real bad and Gaspar had to shoot her!" Tears streamed down her face.

Unsure how to console her, Willy Jo put his arm lightly about her shoulder. "Horsefiddles. I'm sorry. I didn't know."

Vanda Mae hung her head. When she faced him again, her words tumbled out unbridled. "Springer was my best friend. She knew me better than anybody. I don't know what I'm going to do without her!"

Willy Jo resisted the urge to tighten his arm about her while he searched for a comforting reply. "You've still got Tassie, and Firelight, and . . ." He couldn't count a horse as skittish as Hurricane among her assets. " . . . and a couple dozen other horses in your daddy's pasture."

"It's not the same," Vanda Mae mumbled, once again wiping her face on her shirt sleeve. "I've never been so fond of a horse as I was of Springer."

Willy Jo pulled his handkerchief from his back pocket and handed it to her. "I know what you mean."

She pushed his arm off her shoulder. "No, you don't! Not a few minutes ago you were ready to *shoot* a horse!"

"That was just my temper talking! I'd never hurt a horse." He patted Hurricane's shoulder, then glanced at the stable. "I've got work to do. Daddy was expecting me in the lower pasture with that manure long ago. He'll have my hide if I don't get there, and soon, I tell you!"

CHAPTER 2

Still reluctant to head home, Vanda Mae followed Willy Jo toward the stable, hitched Hurricane to the fence post outside, then wandered in and down the center aisle. Beyond the stalls of the roans that were Mr. Winthrop's driving horses was a box containing a horse she'd never seen before—a dark chestnut mare that didn't look like the hacks to which she was accustomed.

She spoke as she stroked its thick mane. "Who are you? You're a right pretty one, aren't you?" The horse had an unusual blaze on its face, a narrow streak of white that flared distinctively on the right side. A sprinkle of white hairs salted her brow line.

Willy Jo came out of the tack room, new tugs looped over his shoulder. "That's April, my new Morgan. I bought her last week. Mama doesn't know it yet, but she's going to enter 'Best Lady Rider' for the first time in twenty years at the Forsyth County Fair this fall, and she's going to win on April!"

"Not a chance!" Vanda Mae challenged. "Now that they've redrawn the county line to include Tanglewood,

I'll be entering your fair, and you know Springer—" she stopped herself short. Swallowing hard, she turned to April again, her words a mere whisper. "You just might win at that, girl. You just might."

"April has a lot to learn, but she's already showing great promise as a jumper. Horsefiddles! She'll be taking a four-foot rail in no time!"

The horse began nibbling on Willy Jo's hair. He laughed. "You want to be brushed, don't you girl?"

April nickered.

"All right, but only for a minute."

He set down the tugs, entered the box stall and began stroking her with a soft brush. As Vanda Mae watched, she noticed another distinguishing feature about the mare—that she had three white socks. Only the left rear leg was completely chestnut.

Not five minutes had lapsed when Willy Jo's daddy marched into the stable, his flaming red sideburns accenting the cross look on his face.

"Willy Jo!"

He tossed the brush aside, hurried out of the stall, and picked up the tugs.

"Is this what they teach you about farmin' at agricultural college? How to shirk your chores to brush that fancy ridin' horse of yours?"

Willy Jo's face reddened. "No, sir."

"I told you I wanted to spread manure on the lower pasture this afternoon. Now, I find the wagon upset, manure all over the drive, and the new team nibblin' on the tulip poplars. What've you got to say for yourself?"

Vanda Mae spoke up. "It's my fault, Mr. Winthrop. Hurricane—"

His angry gaze remained locked on Willy Jo. "I declare, when you come back from school, it's as if you've forgot what it means to work."

"I'm sorry about the manure, Daddy. I'll—"

"Ya graduated agricultural college, bought a fancy horse, and it seems to me you've spent nearly all your time fussin' over her. I've a mind to sell her just so's I can get a good day's labor out of ya!"

Willy Jo's response was firm, but respectful. "I only ride her evenings when my chores are done, sir."

Jabe Winthrop took the tugs from Willy Jo. "Fetch a couple of pitch forks and get Lincoln to help ya." He referred to his farm hand. "I want that load of manure in the lower pasture in an hour." He pulled a bent card from his pocket. "And I'm callin' this Danvers fellow we met at the auction and tellin' him this Morgan mare is for sale."

"But, Daddy, she belongs to me!"

"Not till you've paid back the money ya borrowed from me to buy her!" He strode away.

Vanda Mae went after him. "Mr. Winthrop, sir, don't trouble yourself calling that fellow. My daddy will buy April for me. How much do you want?"

He turned to her, a set look on his face, and named a figure. "That's what was paid for her plus ten percent. Pay before tomorrow or I'll sell to Danvers."

"I'll have the money to you, Mr. Winthrop. I promise!"

Without a word, he tramped out of the stable.

Vanda Mae turned to Willy Jo. "I'm sorry—"

The flush on his face deepened. "Go home, Vannie-Mae, and take April with you! Her blanket, bridle, and saddle are hanging in the tack room." He stepped past her.

Vanda Mae followed him. "I can't take April. She's not paid for."

Willy Jo paused to face her. "Horsefiddles! Your daddy's got to see what he's buying. You can save him the trip over here." He nudged her in the direction of the tack room. When she hesitated, he said, "Better for you to have her than some fool who'll ruin her with a severe bit and a heavy hand. I saw how Danvers treats horses at that auction, and I'd never let him near April. Now take her and git!"

As he walked out the door, she said, "I'll make it up to you, Willy Jo! I promise!"

~~~

Dark clouds were beginning to gather by the time Vanda Mae had ridden home to the stable where Springer had lain ill. She cross-tied the new horse in the center aisle while she removed her saddle and bridle.

Springer's stall was empty now. Gaspar had evidently gone about the business of disposing of her remains, so Vanda Mae thoroughly cleaned and disinfected the loose box and led April to her new quarters. After filling the manger with corn and the rack with hay, she headed for

Tassie's box on the way out to check on the mother-in-waiting.

Even from a distance the sight of her almost made Vanda Mae cry. Tassie's coloring was nearly identical to her sister, Springer—chestnut with a white diamond on her forehead. Could she ever look at the mare and not be reminded of the horse she'd lost? As she approached the foaling box, she tried to console herself with the knowledge that at least she still had Springer's sister, and after two unsuccessful attempts at breeding, would soon have her foal to help chase away today's sorrow.

Drawing nearer, she noticed the mare was dripping with sweat and her stall showed evidence of intestinal complaint. These symptoms, along with the way she shifted from one side of her box to the other, reminded Vanda Mae of Springer when she had first taken ill. Panic rose within.

She patted Tassie's neck. "Easy, girl, easy now. I'll get you some oil." She started toward the tack room as fast as her feet could carry her, running headlong into Gaspar and nearly falling into an empty manger.

He caught her by the shoulders to set her right. "Slow down, little one! What's the hurry?"

"Tassie's sick—just like Springer was! We have to give her oil!"

"Not so fast. Let Gaspar see."

When she returned with him to Tassie's stall, the horse was more skittish than before. Just as Gaspar was about to enter her box, she let loose a huge stream of fluid from her hind quarters.

Vanda Mae knew from the blood-tinged color it wasn't urine. Her heart raced. "Gaspar, help her! Don't let her die!"

Cautiously, he entered the box. Inspecting Tassie's underside and the discharge, he exited the stall and focused on Vanda Mae. "Tassie's not sick." A smile spread on his ruddy, narrow face. "She's ready to have her baby!"

Vanda Mae wanted to laugh and cry at the same time. Then a new worry took over. "We must help her! What do we do?"

Gaspar took off his straw hat and wiped his damp forehead on his sleeve. "We can do nothing but wait, little one. Tassie knows what to do."

Vanda Mae watched as Tassie lay down and began to strain, stood up again, then repeated the process. The horse's actions seemed exacerbated by the rumble of an approaching storm. Gaspar spoke soothingly in Spanish but Tassie showed no sign of calming down.

Vanda Mae's apprehension increased. She paced across the center aisle and back. "Tassie's in trouble, Gaspar, I just know it!"

He regarded her sternly. "*Senorita*, do not fuss!"

"But she's—"

"You are upsetting her! If you cannot watch calmly then go to the house and I will fetch you when she is finished."

"Go to the house? Never!" Vanda Mae instantly regretted her words. "Forgive me, Gaspar. I'm jumpy as a hay bug from all that's happened today." Silently, she prayed, *Lord, please keep me quiet. And please help Tassie deliver her foal! Thank you!*

Tassie continued to get up and down, straining harder and harder. Rain began beating down on the stable roof. When several minutes had passed and the mare was lying on her side, a shiny membrane began to appear below her tail.

Gaspar put his fingers to his lips, then took Vanda Mae by the hand and opened the door of the box. In a low tone, he said, "Do you see the sack and the front feet inside?"

Vanda Mae nodded. One foot was positioned ahead of the other.

Gaspar continued. "This is good. Tassie will have a normal birth."

No sooner had he spoken than a clap of thunder boomed overhead. The mare strained violently, expelling more of the membrane. The nose, head, and chest of the foal came into view.

Gaspar knelt down a safe distance from Tassie inviting Vanda Mae to do the same. "Watch closely," he told her. "The foal will break the sack and start to breathe."

Minutes later, when the storm had quieted, it happened just as he said. Then Tassie became more violent than ever. Vanda Mae clutched Gaspar's arm with one hand and pressed the other over her mouth.

With her baby half born, Tassie took a short rest. Then giving a fierce effort, she pushed forth the foal's hips and hind quarters, except for the rear legs.

With the mare again at rest, Gaspar led Vanda Mae out of the box and closed the door. "We must let Tassie be. If she gets too quickly to her feet, her little one could die."

Awed by what she had seen, Vanda Mae continued to watch in silence. The thunderstorm over, sunshine peeked through the window. A few moments later the foal's hind feet appeared. Soon after that, Tassie rose. The cord attaching her to her baby broke, then she settled down beside her little one.

Vanda Mae was so touched by the sight of mama and baby nose to nose getting their first real look at one another, she couldn't have spoken a word even if she'd wanted to. Instantly, she fell in love with the tiny horse who also bore the colorings of her kin—a tiny diamond-shaped patch of white on her chestnut forehead. The prospect of caring for it and watching it grow so dominated her thoughts, she was hardly aware of the dinner bell ringing in the distance. Glancing at Gaspar, she saw that he was smiling as proudly as if he were the new arrival's daddy even though he'd witnessed many such births in his years at Tanglewood, and with the circus horses before that.

He spoke quietly. "This is the most important moment in the little one's life, when it learns who its mama is."

Tassie undertook a thorough washing of her foal from the white marking on its face to legs so spindly they seemed almost ugly. When she reached the newborn's hind quarters, Vanda Mae realized that the newcomer was a female. "I have the perfect name for Tassie's foal," she announced. "Jewel, for the diamond on her forehead."

"Jewel," Gaspar repeated with a nod.

When the filly tried unsuccessfully to gain her feet, Vanda Mae said, "I hope she'll be a jumper in a few years. Until then at least I have—" She caught herself short. "Gracious! In all the excitement about Tassie, I forgot to tell you about April!" She was about to lead him to the opposite end of the stable when the dark-skinned maid—once nanny for her and Rosalie—appeared at the door, her hands set on her wide hips.

"Miss Vanda! Mr. Gaspar! I done rung the dinner bell long ago!" she announced.

"Don't scold, Shani," Vanda Mae begged. "We've been watching the most amazing miracle take place." She beckoned the woman to Tassie's stall.

Shani focused on Tassie and Jewel and drew a sharp breath. "My, my, my. Ain't they a pretty sight? Now I know why nobody come to dinner."

"Do you think you could possibly bring it to us?" Vanda Mae pleaded. "Jewel hasn't yet made it to her feet, and I'd hate to miss seeing her take her mother's milk for the very first time."

Shani thought a moment, then a smile appeared. "Miss Vanda, you're the spoiled rottenest child this side of the Atlantic Ocean. But I suppose I can bring you and Mr. Gaspar each a plate of dinner."

She'd turned to leave when Vanda Mae remembered April. "Shani, wait! I've got something I want you and Gaspar to see." She led them to April's stall. "Isn't she beautiful? And she's all mine."

Gaspar's brow wrinkled. "Is she not the new Morgan of the Winthrops?"

"Was," Vanda Mae informed him, adding proudly, "now April's all mine." To Shani, she said, "Did Daddy tell you what time he'll be home tonight? We need to take the payment for April to Mr. Winthrop."

"Your daddy done caught the train to Durham this mornin', child. Said to remind you he won't be back till tomorrow night."

Vanda Mae inhaled sharply. "Tomorrow night? But—"

Gaspar spoke up. "Surely, payment can wait until then."

Vanda Mae made no reply. Mr. Winthrop's angry words rang in her head. *Pay before tomorrow or I'll sell her to Danvers.*

CHAPTER 3

The sun had been up for three hours when Vanda Mae gave in to exhaustion and lay down on a mound of straw near Tassie's foaling box. The instant her eyes closed, scenes passed through her mind of Jewel refusing to nurse, then becoming sicker and weaker with septicemia as the night wore on. How thankful she was that the veterinarian had responded to Gaspar's midnight telephone plea.

Silently, she prayed, *Dear Lord, bless Doc Whitehead for coming out in the middle of the night with the medicine. And thank you that he was able to persuade Jewel to nurse. Now please make Tassie's foal well and strong!*

Within seconds, Vanda Mae fell fast asleep. She was unsure how long she'd slept when loud voices at the other end of the stable woke her. Getting to her feet, she saw Mr. Winthrop arguing with Gaspar outside April's stall while another man—a stranger wearing a tall white hat with a wide black band—inspected the mare. She caught Jabe Winthrop's heated words as she hurried toward him.

"Don't you tell me the girl wants the Morgan!" He jabbed the air with his driving whip. "If she did, she'd have paid for the horse last night!"

"Please believe. Miss Foxe want this animal ver' much. Last night she—"

Vanda Mae cut in. "I was up all night with a very sick foal, Mr. Winthrop. I'm sorry I didn't deliver the money to you. I meant to call and tell you Daddy will bring it when he gets home from Durham tonight."

The stranger in April's stall spoke up. "Mr. Winthrop, I'd like to saddle up your Morgan and see how she rides."

Jabe turned to Gaspar. "Ya heard Mr. Danvers. Fetch her saddle."

Gaspar backed away. "Respectfully, sir, I do no work for you." He pivoted and walked out of the stable.

Jabe grumbled, then addressed Vanda Mae. "Ya took April. Now go and get her bridle and saddle like a good little girl."

She smiled. "It's hanging in the tack room, sir." She hurried after Gaspar who was headed for the rig Danvers had parked outside the stable. The hired hand was looking closely at the black gelding hitched to the buggy when Vanda Mae caught up with him. "What is it, Gaspar?"

He didn't reply. Instead, he spoke softly to the horse, peeling back its lips to inspect its mouth. Then he walked around to the right side. There, he pointed to a fresh mark on the horse's hind quarters. "Just as I thought. Danvers makes much use of his whip. And this horse's mouth is scarred."

He continued his inspection until Danvers came out of the stable atop the Morgan, immediately digging his heels into her flanks. Jabe Winthrop stood just outside the door watching the man put the animal through her paces, making frequent use of his riding crop as he switched her lead from one side to the other.

Vanda Mae strode up to Willy Jo's father. *"Please* don't sell to that man," she pleaded. "He'll be too hard on April."

Winthrop's gaze remained on the horse and rider. "A tap on the hind quarters now and then can't hurt the animal, Vanda Mae."

Gaspar spoke up. "The Morgan needs gentling, not whipping."

Jabe smiled cynically. "That's a matter of opinion."

Danvers cut this way and that across the meadow, using his riding crop against the Morgan with every change of direction. Vanda Mae was itching to argue further with Willy Jo's father about his decision to sell to such a man. Just when she thought she would lose the battle with her tongue, Willy Jo came tearing into the pasture atop one of his father's roans, heading straight for Danvers. Though she was too far away to hear their conversation, it was evident from Willy Jo's gesticulations that the exchange was heated. Moments later, they rode up to the stable and dismounted, hitching their horses to the fence rail.

Willy Jo marched up to his father, Danvers close behind. "Why didn't you tell me you were coming here to sell April out from under Vannie-Mae?"

"Couldn't see the point in gettin' ya riled. How'd ya find out?"

"Linc—" Willy Jo interrupted himself. "Doesn't matter. I came to stop you from selling to this man."

Despite the ruddiness flooding his cheeks, Jabe remained calm. "It's not your decision to make, son."

Willy Jo pressed further. "What do you know about this man except that he came to the auction, bid up the price on the horse we wanted, then handed you a card with a number to call in case you changed your mind about April?"

Jabe replied in a taut, low voice. "What I know is this man wants the horse, he's got the money, and I'm gonna take it!"

Danvers spoke up. "I'm glad reason prevails. I'm ready to deal." He pulled a roll of currency from his pocket and began peeling off bills.

Willy Jo stopped him with an upward cut of his hand. "Put your money away, Mr. Danvers. They ought to make it illegal for the likes of you to own a horse!"

Danvers seemed unruffled. "Ain't—hasn't your daddy ever warned you not to make accusations against a stranger, young Winthrop?"

"You're no stranger to Doc Whitehead. I won't repeat in front of Vannie-Mae what *he* said about some horses you sold down in Davidson County!"

Jabe turned on his son. "When did you talk to Doc Whitehead?"

"I rang him up not half an hour ago after Lincoln told me that lame sow was looking worse."

When his father waved off the problem, Danvers spoke again. "With all due respect, young Winthrop, I ain't— haven't ever met this Whitehead fella, or solicited his services. His accusations against me are false."

Vanda Mae didn't believe Danvers for a second, and was about to say so when Jabe spoke instead.

"Doc Whitehead is mistaken!"

Gaspar spoke up. "Mr. Winthrop, sir, the good doctor makes no mistake, of this I am certain. If he says that Mr. Danvers is unkind to horses, then—"

Jabe turned on him. "You stay out of this, ya circus riffraff!" To Danvers, he said, "If ya want the horse, she's yours."

Willy Jo stiffened. "I bought April and I won't let Danvers have her!"

"You'll do as I say unless ya can pay off the loan I gave ya!"

Despite his father's words, Willy Jo led April toward the stable.

Jabe pursued. "Just where do ya think you're goin'?"

Willy Jo paused. "This is April's new home. You'll have your money as soon as Mr. Foxe returns from Durham."

Jabe shook his finger at Willy Jo. "If April stays here, then *you* do, too. Ya can pick up your belongin's tonight when ya bring me my money. And ya'd better start lookin' for a job on somebody else's farm 'cause you're off my payroll for good!" He strode away.

A minute later, Danvers and Jabe Winthrop drove off taking the roan Willy Jo had arrived on with them.

The look on Willy Jo's face tore at Vanda Mae. She searched for words of comfort. "It will all work out, Willy Jo. By tonight you'll have your loan paid off and your daddy will want you home again."

He shook his head thoughtfully. "Fiddles, Vannie-Mae. Daddy and I, we've been having our differences for quite some time. He meant what he said about moving out."

Vanda Mae drew a slow breath. "I'm going to pray God will soften his heart and change his mind."

CHAPTER 4

Willy Jo unbuttoned his collar as Mr. Foxe drove the both of them out of Salem and headed home at the end of another hot week at his lumber yard. Despite Vanda Mae's prayers, and his own, three and a half long weeks had passed since he'd seen his daddy or his home—three and a half weeks since Mr. Foxe had offered shelter at Tanglewood and a position at Foxe Brothers selling lumber, cement, shingles, and other building supplies.

The lengthy drive to and from work seemed at first an undue burden. Like many others, Willy Jo hadn't understood Mr. Foxe's preference to spend a significant amount of time on the road traveling to and from his country estate each day, rather than staying week nights in the city. Now, after nearly a month in Mr. Foxe's employ and in residence at his horse farm, Willy Jo knew the reasons. Evenings at Tanglewood, free of city noise and traffic, were next to heaven after dealing with construction schedules, supply problems, and customer demands. And the winding route home, over hills and through woods, offered a release all its own when taken in a fine buggy drawn by a handsome team, strong and fresh and ready for the challenge.

The long drive also afforded Willy Jo plenty of time to think. Though he longed desperately to return to his father's farm, the instant he considered it, his stomach soured. He didn't miss the arguments, the criticisms, the constant reminders that he couldn't do anything well enough to please his daddy. And he would never apologize for refusing to sell April to Eck Danvers.

Mr. Foxe interrupted his thoughts. "I saw your daddy today."

The words, "Did he ask about me?" slipped out before Willy Jo could stop them.

It seemed like a long time before Mr. Foxe replied. "We had a pleasant conversation about you. I told him what a fine job you've been doing since you came to work for me. Told him if he has need of you on his farm, you're in no way obligated to remain in my employ."

Willy Jo couldn't help wishing that just once he'd heard his own father tell him what a fine job he was doing, but it was a foolish fancy. From the sounds of it, his daddy hadn't even wanted to know how he was.

Mr. Foxe continued. "Son, I know you and I come from different customs where our church-going is concerned. But we pray to the same God. He can smooth out the troubles with your daddy."

Willy Jo's warm face grew even hotter. "With all due respect, sir, I've prayed every prayer I could think of since you took me in, but from the sounds of it, nothing's changed where my daddy's concerned."

Mr. Foxe laid a hand on his shoulder. "We both need to keep praying."

Willy Jo bit his tongue to keep from asking what good it would do. Weary of the problem with his father, he turned his thoughts in a different direction. At least some good had come of his troubles. Vanda Mae was enjoying her new horse. Watching her ride April, and mounting the horse himself after dinner each evening to ride across Foxe's four-hundred-acre estate with Vanda Mae and her daddy were two small pleasures he anticipated at the end of the day.

A third pleasure was seeing Tassie's baby grow strong. He relished the sight of the mare and filly romping in the pasture. He was anticipating the scene when Mr. Foxe turned up the drive to find Vanda Mae mounted on Hurricane.

"Daddy, dinner won't be ready for at least an hour. Shani had to go to Winston, to Uncle George and Aunt Ophelia's to see Pearl. She's only just come home." She named her father's brother and his wife, the employers of Shani's oldest daughter who was suffering a difficult pregnancy—the same aunt and uncle with whom Vanda Mae and Rosalie had lived during the school year to attend Salem Academy with their cousin, Lida Jean.

Mr. Foxe scowled. "Pearl didn't have her baby already, did she?"

Vanda Mae shook her head. "False alarm. With dinner so late, I thought the three of us could ride now. By the time we've finished eating, it'll be too dark. Besides, I plan to write to Rosalie after dinner."

Mr. Foxe smiled. "You and Willy Jo go ahead. I'm going to take my bath *before* dinner, for a change."

While Willy Jo changed into riding breeches, Vanda Mae saddled April. Soon, he boarded her and headed for his favorite path beside the Yadkin River. Vanda Mae followed him for awhile, then continued on ahead when he dismounted to sit by the water and watch it flow past. She'd been gone only a minute or two when he had the eerie feeling someone was lurking nearby.

"Vannie-Mae?"

He scanned the woods. Finding no sign of her, he hitched April to a tree limb and stretched out on the river bank, leaning back against a tree stump.

He relished these rare moments of solitude. Putting away thoughts of his father, he contemplated the nature of the place—the gentle sway of green rushes and silver reeds, the smell of the muskrats, the low buzz of dragon fly wings as they darted hither and yon. Even the song of the cicadas improved when muted by the wild grape vines and holly along the banks.

He left these thoughts at the unmistakable sound of Vanda Mae riding toward him as she kept up a patter of one-way conversation with Hurricane. He watched her through the trees. How pretty she sat atop the grey gelding. Her long hair was caught to the side in a blue satin ribbon. He was glad she hadn't gone the way of most girls at sixteen, piling her long tresses atop her head, for he like the way they bounced against her shirt with each step of her horse. Her shoulders were square, her back straight and leaning slightly forward from her narrow waist. Only her toes were in the stirrup leaving her heels angled sharply down in the way of a good rider in a hunt seat. He'd told himself his rides with her and her daddy were borne strictly of the pleasure he derived from good horseflesh and his love of the river but he hadn't been completely honest. He valued the friendship he was developing with Vanda Mae, and the growing respect between him and her daddy.

As the young girl came closer, her lighthearted horse chat ended. She wore a contemplative expression as she dismounted, set her hands on her hips, and marched over to where he was resting.

"Willy Jo Winthrop, why don't you just go home and take April with you!"

He sprang to his feet, words of protestation on his tongue, but she continued.

"The only reason you're staying at Tanglewood is because of that horse. Well, you can have her back! I don't want her any—"

"Vannie-Mae Foxe, hush up!"

Her jaw clamped shut.

He wagged his finger. "You don't know a thing about me, or you'd have figured out why I'm still at Tanglewood. But I'll tell you this. It doesn't have much to do with April!"

"It has *everything* to do with April! And your daddy."

"Not quite."

"Why did he insist on selling her? Tell me that!"

Willy Jo sighed. "Because we don't get along. Haven't gotten along in years."

"Then you ought to start."

"It's not that simple."

"Why not? You just walk up to your daddy and say, 'From now on, we ought to get along.'"

He started to chuckle. "You're crazy as a Betsy bug!"

"Am not! It makes perfect sense!"

He laughed harder and she joined in.

Moments later, she said, "That's the first time I've heard you laugh since the day you came here to stay. You ought to make a habit of it, Willy Jo. You're much more pleasant to be around when you're in good humor."

"So are you. Now do me a favor. Sit down and be still so I can rest a mite longer. Goodness knows I've put in a hard week at your daddy's business." He stretched out as he had been before she came.

She chose a spot close to the water a few feet away from him. Fidgeting with a grape vine, she began picking leaves and tossing them in the Yadkin.

Willy Jo watched her through slitted eyes. Her mouth was naturally upturned even in thought, and her movements graceful. This fascination for the younger Foxe girl caused him shame over his heart's betrayal. If Rosalie were here, would he be distracted by her younger sister?

His ponderings reached no conclusion for they were interrupted by the sound of the dinner bell ringing in the distance—Shani's warning that her meal would be served soon and they must head to the barn. He expected Vanda Mae to challenge him to a race back to the stable, but she remained silent as she boarded Hurricane, and instead of trotting, kept her pace to a walk, staying even with him as they crossed the large meadow leading up to the stable.

He sensed something unusual in the way Gaspar was waiting for them outside the stable door. The hired hand knew they enjoyed unsaddling their own horses after a ride, but he reached for Hurricane's rein, then April's, his dark eyes sparkling.

"Shani wishes you both to go to the house at once. I will take care of your horses tonight."

Vanda Mae climbed down. "But why can't—"

Gaspar cut her off. *"Señorita* Foxe, please do as I say. *Pronto!"*

With a shrug of her shoulders she headed for the manor house. Willy Jo caught up with her, holding open the door to the back room. Much to his surprise, they found themselves face to face with Mrs. Foxe. Mother and daughter eagerly embraced.

"Mama, what are you doing here? I didn't expect to see you till the end of August!"

Standing back, Mrs. Foxe's focus turned to Willy Jo. "I guess I couldn't wait that long."

At that moment, his mother and younger brother— who'd grown an inch since he'd left for the mountains— entered the room. Before Willy Jo could even greet them, Vanda Mae was in a flurry.

"Bobby Dan! Come outside! You've got to see Tassie's foal!"

When they had left, Willy Jo took his mother's hands in his, aware of her careworn look. "Hello, Mama. This is a surprise."

"I've come to take you home with me and Bobby Dan."

Willy Jo released her hands, lowering his gaze. "I can't go. Not yet."

"Then drive me and Bobby Dan home and at least say hello to your father."

Looking directly into her sad eyes, he said, "I'm sorry. I can't."

She sighed. "That's going to make things mighty awkward come Sunday, Willy Jo."

He waited to hear her explanation, but the opportunity vanished when Mr. Foxe joined them. Looking refreshed from his bath, he put his arm about his wife's waist as he addressed Willy Jo's mother. "Welcome back, Virginia. I understand you-all are going to be here for Sunday dinner." Giving his wife a squeeze, he added, "Do you realize this is the first time in years our two families will be together on Minnie's birthday?"

Feeling trapped, Willy Jo backed away. "I won't be here, sir. It would spoil the party. Now, if you'll excuse me?" He'd taken but one step toward the door when Mr. Foxe stopped him.

"Son, these ladies have been fretting about you since the day you left home. They've come back from the mountains strictly on your account. The least you can do is lend them your presence at Sunday dinner."

Willy Jo thought a moment, then swallowed hard. "All right, sir. I'll be here." He silently added, *but it's a recipe for disaster.*

Virginia smiled. "Thank you, son. Now, are you sure you won't drive me and Bobby Dan home?"

When he made no immediate reply, Mr. Foxe said, "Gaspar will do it. In fact," he paused to glance out the window, "he's bringing the buggy around this very minute."

With a flick of her hand, Virginia told Willy Jo, "Go and fetch your brother, will you?"

He ducked out the back door. His brother was doing a handstand on the top rail of the fence that enclosed the pasture while Vanda Mae applauded. Willy Jo gave a whistle—the three-note call he and his brother had used from childhood—and they immediately started toward him.

As they drew near, Willy Jo couldn't help feeling a trifle piqued at his brother's continuous showing off—now running ahead of Vanda Mae to do three handsprings in succession, then making an about face to perform three more, landing face to face with her. She laughed at his antics and gave him a shove which sent him into another round of handsprings.

Impatient, Willy Jo whistled once more. His brother said something to Vanda Mae, then headed toward him while she stayed behind.

Bobby Dan's new height was reflected in his assertive attitude toward Willy Jo. "You'd better make your peace with Daddy come Sunday, 'cause I've got no desire to spend the rest of my summer on the farm." He stomped off toward the drive before Willy Jo could reply.

Vanda Mae joined him, her enthusiasm for Bobby Dan obvious. "Did you see your brother's acrobatics? He says he's been practicing day and night!"

She rambled on until they reached the drive where his mother stood in conversation with Vanda Mae's parents beside the carriage.

Willy Jo's mother put her gloved finger to her lips and touched it to his cheek. "See you Sunday, son. I'm counting on you not to let anything spoil Mrs. Foxe's birthday party."

He nodded, helping her into the carriage. Bobby Dan climbed in beside her, sparing Willy Jo neither a word nor a glance. Instead, he pulled a clown face for Vanda Mae who giggled like a child as Gaspar drove away.

CHAPTER 5

The perspiration on Willy Jo's brow came from more than the summer heat as the buggy carrying his father, brother, and mother pulled to a halt in front of the Foxe home for Sunday dinner. Though he went out with Mr. and Mrs. Foxe and Vanda Mae to greet his family, his father made no acknowledgement of his presence until the others headed indoors.

Taking Willy Jo aside, his father told him, "I'm only here to please your mother." A reviling look in his eye, he added, "Far as I'm concerned, we've got nothin' to say to one another." He paused to discharge a wad of spit inches from the toe of Willy Jo's polished boot, then turned on his heel and headed for the house.

~~~

At the dinner table, Vanda Mae soon grew tired of listening to Willy Jo's younger brother tell how he and his cohorts at Blowing Rock had squandered their time playing practical jokes. They had entered the town office late at night, removed the Independence Day fireworks, and set them off a day early. They had picked the lock on the hotel linen closet, removed all the clean bed linens, and hid them in the stable so the chambermaids couldn't do their work. And they had stolen all the carrots and apples from the locked pantry and fed them to their favorite horses.

In conclusion, Bobby Dan informed her, "I had more fun this year than I've ever had at Blowing Rock, and I have you to thank for it—you and Gaspar—for teaching me how to open locks."

Vanda Mae stiffened. "I'm ashamed of you, Bobby Dan—ashamed that you would put such knowledge to ill purposes! We only showed you how to open locks for the amusement of your friends, not so you'd commit vandalism."

"They were amused, all right!"

Mr. Winthrop laughed. "Boyish pranks, that's all it was, Vanda Mae. Innocent, boyish pranks. If you had a brother, you'd be more understandin'."

She bit back the retort that was on her tongue and stabbed another piece of ham, thankful that her father took conversation in a new direction, extolling the virtues of Willy Jo and his newly acquired skills in the lumber yard business.

~~~

Despite Mr. Foxe's compliments, Willy Jo sensed beyond all doubt that his daddy didn't care to hear about his eldest son's virtues. When birthday cake had been served and consumed and the meal finally ended, Willy Jo wanted nothing more than to saddle April for a ride to the river where he could sit all by himself, but Mr. Foxe made a different proposal as they were rising from the dinner table.

"Jabe, let's you and me and your boys set a spell in the library. It's the coolest room in the house, it ought to be tolerable."

Daddy pulled a cigar from his pocket. "This and some more lemonade will make it bearable."

Despite the heat in the library, Willy Jo felt frozen out by his father's continued attention to Bobby Dan. A moment of relief came in the form of Vanda Mae when she delivered a pitcher of fresh lemonade. The sympathetic look in her eyes assured him that at least one person in the house understood his plight.

A few minutes later, his father blew smoke rings into the air, knocked ashes off his cigar, and said contemplatively, "Bobby Dan, there's somethin' I've been meanin' to discuss with ya, now that you're home from Blowin' Rock. It's time ya took up more responsibilities on the farm—workin' full time from now until school starts up again." To Mr. Foxe, he said, "I think he's ready to become a partner in the hog farmin' business, don't you?"

Mr. Foxe shrugged. "That's a family matter, Jabe."

Willy Jo felt deeply wounded by the knowledge that his father intended to replace him on the farm—and with the son who truly disdained the farming life.

His younger brother made quick work of his lemonade, set his empty glass on the tray, and moved to the edge of his chair. "If you all will excuse me, I need some fresh air."

Jabe said, "But son, we need to—"

Bobby Dan cut him off. "Later, Daddy." On his way out the door, he sent Willy Jo a piercing look with a message that read, *You'd better settle your differences with Daddy and come home. You know I hate farming!*

He was no sooner gone than Jabe took up conversation again. "Bobby Dan's my clever boy. He's really gonna amount to somethin' one day."

Mr. Foxe reiterated his earlier praise. "And Willy Jo has picked up on the building supply business in no time, Jabe. You can be mighty proud of the way he handles himself."

Willy Jo set his glass down so abruptly, he spilled lemonade on the tray. "With all due respect Mr. Foxe, Daddy, I won't sit and listen while the two of you discuss me as if I weren't here."

~~~

Vanda Mae was in the parlor with her mother and Mrs. Winthrop discussing the happy news that Shani's daughter had given birth to a healthy baby girl just hours ago when Willy Jo strode past. The way his heels thudded down the hall—despite the cushion of the oriental runner—caused a momentary lull in conversation. Certain Willy Jo was escaping tension in the library by heading out to ride April, and eager to join him, Vanda Mae spoke up.

"Mrs. Winthrop, Mama, it's about time for a Sunday afternoon horseback ride. Care to join me?" Though in cooler weather the three of them had often ridden together—sometimes in the company of her daddy and the Winthrop men—she prayed a little prayer that today, the women would decline.

Her mother answered with a flick of her hand. "You go on, honey. We're not done talking."

Vanda Mae hurried upstairs to change into her riding breeches. She was on her way to the stable, passing the fence where Bobby Dan was practicing hand stands, when he dropped down beside her.

"Vanda Mae, I was talking with a friend of mine yesterday, Porky Steadman. You know him, don't you?"

Without a pause, she continued toward the stable, Bobby Dan close at hand. "I think his daddy buys lumber from my daddy," she acknowledged with disinterest.

"Well, he and some of the other poor suffering fools who haven't gone away for the summer are getting up a party for Friday night—a trolley party. The Twin City Concert Band is going to be in the second car, and when we get to Hotel Quincy, there'll be some great refreshments. You'll go with me, won't you?"

She stopped to gaze up at the fair-haired, blue-eyed fellow who had been her closest childhood friend—the Winthrop she had always considered to be the better-looking, more amusing, more congenial of the two—and came to a startling conclusion. "Bobby Dan, there was a time when I'd have consented in an instant, but I've discovered something about you today. I no longer care to be in your company."

A dark look flashed across his face as she walked away. An instant later he was turning handsprings, halting directly in front of her to pull a clown face so contorted she almost smiled. When she tried to walk around him, he danced back and forth refusing to let her pass, constantly changing his expression until he looked so completely absurd the corners of her mouth drew upward.

His triumphant look matched his words. "I knew I could make you smile! Now say you'll come with me on Friday night."

Smile vanishing, she glared at him. "I'm not happy about you, Bobby Dan. And I'm not going with you. Find someone else."

He followed her into the stable. "What is it with you all of a sudden, Vanda Mae?"

She took Hurricane's halter and lead from the peg in the tack room and turned to face him. "You've changed, Bobby Dan. You're not the nice person you used to be. Your behavior at Blowing Rock this summer is inexcusable."

When she tried to walk away he trapped her against the wall, placing his hands either side of her head. His look was genuinely contrite. "I'm sorry, Vanda Mae. Truly, I never meant to offend you by what I did. I hope you can find it in your heart to forgive me."

She ducked beneath his arm. "I don't hold grudges, Bobby Dan. I just don't feel a desire for your company."

He matched his stride to hers as she headed for the pasture. "I almost forgot to tell you, Porky Steadman's daddy bought a fancy new thoroughbred—finest horse you ever want to see. She was a winner at Saratoga two years back. If you go with me Friday night, I'll fix it so you get to ride her on Saturday."

She offered a skeptical look. "Don't add fibbing to your list of transgressions, Bobby Dan. There's no way I'm going to believe a winning thoroughbred from Saratoga, New York, wound up in Mr. Steadman's possession and is now his saddle horse."

Bobby Dan raised his hands in protest. "I'm not fibbing! She'd leave your Hurricane in a cloud of dust! Say you'll go to the party, and you'll find out I speak the truth."

She gazed at Hurricane, several yards away from her in the pasture, then turned to Bobby Dan. "If Mama and Daddy say it's all right—"

"They'll give permission. My mama's one of the chaperones."

"You'd better not be funning me about Steadman's horse, Bobby Dan, or I won't speak to you for a month!"

"Be ready to leave for Salem at half past six Friday night. We'll drive by to pick you up." He turned one cartwheel, then looked back. "By the way, you'd best not mention the race horse to your folks—not yet, anyhow. Just tell them we're going riding at Steadmans'." He cartwheeled away.

A few minutes later Vanda Mae was astride Hurricane trotting toward the Yadkin. She slowed to a walk as soon as she entered the woods, turning down the path she was certain would lead her to Willy Jo. He was precisely as she'd found him Friday evening, stretched out near a stump while April munched on the leaves of a nearby oak.

Willy Jo gave a start when Hurricane's hoof clacked against a rock. His gaze met Vanda Mae's, and then he got up and moved closer to the water. Obviously, he was in no mood for conversation.

Vanda Mae couldn't blame Willy Jo for preferring his solitude, but neither could she keep to herself the thoughts that had been crowding her mind since she'd left the house. She slid off Hurricane, looped his rein around a red buckeye sapling and strode right up to Willy Jo.

"I was wrong the other night, and you were right. It was perfectly ridiculous of me to suggest that you could get along with your daddy."

He simply looked at her. In the silence, a red-winged blackbird began to scold. A mockingbird repeated the sound, then a crow gave an even louder opinion.

He chuckled. "Fiddles, Vannie-Mae! Do you realize you've just walked into a perfectly serene piece of the forest and started an argument among the birds?"

She laughed, then plopped down on the stump. "At least I didn't start an argument with you this time."

He half-smiled, then gazed out at the river as if his thoughts were miles away, though she was sure they wandered no farther than the library at Tanglewood.

Her own thoughts remained even closer at hand, focused on the fellow beside her. She was enjoying having an honorary "big brother" at Tanglewood more than she wanted to admit. He was as interested in horses as she and her daddy were, and eager to ride even when her father was too tired. She'd miss Willy Jo if he left, a thought that prompted a question.

"Willy Jo, do you suppose your daddy will ever want you to come home again?"

"Vannie-Mae, now that I've been at Tanglewood awhile, I've got a real yen to find myself a new daddy. One like yours."

The longing in his voice was unmistakable, and his words twisted a wrench in her heart.

CHAPTER 6

Willy Jo sat down in the library to read after dinner, thankful that Friday had arrived and only one more work day remained in the week. He hadn't even finished the front page of the *Winston-Salem Journal* when he heard Vanda Mae's footsteps and the rustling of petticoats as she entered the room. When he lowered the paper, he was astonished by the vision of pure femininity standing before him—a young lady with her hair piled on her head, a satin bow tied about her high collar, and rows of lace ruffle running down the bodice of her pale lavender dress. Surely, she'd be the prettiest thing ever to step on a trolley at the party in Salem tonight.

She crossed the room to perch on the chair next to his. "Don't tell Bobby Dan, but I'd rather be on a horse at Tanglewood than on that trolley in the city tonight."

"Don't go." He delved into the paper once again.

"I can't beg off now! I promised Bobby Dan! Besides, he gave me his word that I'd get to ride that new thoroughbred at the Steadmans' if I go tonight."

Willy Jo punched the paper into a fold and focused on her. "You're fixing to take a fall, Vannie-Mae. Steadmans' horse is only green broke. She's not ready for pleasure riding."

Vanda Mae sighed. "How do you know so much about it?"

"Fiddles, she's the talk of Winston!"

"Well, I'm not afraid to ride her!" With more rustling of taffeta, she flitted from the room.

Willy Jo tossed the paper aside and stepped up to the open window, but the warm, humid breeze did nothing to temper his troubled thoughts. Minutes later, when Bobby Dan rang the bell, he wondered if he should have a talk with his younger brother, but decided against it knowing it would only lead to an argument.

Instead, he wandered into the front hall to simply say hello, and was impressed by Bobby Dan's mature image and demeanor. His brother's blond hair was neatly slicked back making him appear older than his seventeen years, and he'd tied a neat striped bow at his collar—using a tie he'd obviously borrowed from Willy Jo's own collection. He followed the young couple out to the drive, wishing he were going along to help his mother keep an eye on things, but his presence would be an intrusion.

Nevertheless, when he mounted April a quarter of an hour later for his evening ride by the river, he found himself on the road to Salem instead. When he arrived at Academy Square, he had no trouble recognizing the two trolley cars reserved for the party. The front car was lit all around with colored electric lights. Musicians warm-

ing up on their band instruments filled the second car.
Hastily hitching April to the post beside his father's rig,
he climbed aboard the first car and made his way past the
front seats where Vanda Mae, Bobby Dan, Porky Steadman, and their friends were sitting, and settled beside his
mother at the back.

To the tune of *Sweet Rosie O'Grady,* the cars rolled
up Main Street past Douthit's Fancy Goods, Schaffner's
Drug Store, Senseman Company Brooms and Stoves,
Vogler and Sons Furniture and Undertaking, Mrs. Stan-
ton's Millinery Store, and past several of the tobacco
factories and leaf houses in Winston. All along the way
people paused to watch and listen until the trolley came
to a stop at the Hotel Quincy for refreshments.

While the others went inside, Willy Jo stayed on the
empty trolley. He'd never been much good making polite, party conversation, and the prospect of watching
Vanda Mae talking and laughing with Bobby Dan and
their young friends didn't hold appeal. He gazed out the
trolley window watching the carriages pass by, his mind
wandering until he caught a glimpse of a driver wearing
a tall white hat with a wide black band. Leaning out the
window for a better look, he concluded it was Eck Danvers headed down Main Street toward Salem.

The mere sight of the man riled his gut, but Willy Jo
had to reckon with the fact that Eck Danvers alone had
not been the cause of the rift with his daddy. He wanted
badly to smooth over the troubles between them, but despite dozens of prayers and weeks of anguishing over the
problem since his move to Tanglewood, he still hadn't
any idea how reconciliation could be accomplished.

Such concerns took flight as the young people began to fill the trolley car again, ready for their return ride to Academy Square. Minutes later they arrived back at their starting point. While the others were still saying their good-byes, Willy Jo headed for his father's buggy to light the carriage lanterns for the drive home, planning to ride alongside of them on April. But where was she? The Morgan was no longer tied to the post beside his father's rig!

His heart in his throat, he searched the square, hoping she'd only gotten loose and wandered off to graze, but after a thorough investigation including a score of inquiries, he'd found no sign of her.

His mother, brother, and Vanda Mae were waiting in his father's buggy when he returned. Seeing that Bobby Dan had already lit the lanterns, Willy Jo climbed into the front seat beside his mother.

"April's missing."

Vanda Mae's forehead wrinkled. "Where can she be?"

Willy Jo pointed to the hitching post. "I tied her right there, and now she's gone."

His mother said, "Surely she's around here somewhere. Did you—"

"I've asked everyone who parked on this block. No one's seen her."

"I hope this isn't Porky's idea of a joke," said Bobby Dan. "It'd be just like him to—"

Willy Jo cut in. "I spoke with Porky. He hasn't seen her." Pulling away from the curb, he said, "I'm going to drive around the school and take another look, but I think we've got a better chance of sneaking dawn past a rooster than we have of finding April."

Darkness had settled over Salem—and in Willy Jo's heart—by the time he'd finished his tour of the Academy neighborhood. The other occupants of the buggy reflected his grim mood. He set off for Tanglewood, deeply disturbed to be leaving without Vanda Mae's Morgan. His thoughts were in a muddle over who would steal her, and why. He'd driven a couple of miles when several blasts from a shotgun rent the air.

The team lurched, throwing his mother against him and all but tossing his brother and Vanda Mae onto the floor.

Before Willy Jo could calm the roans, a lone rider galloped past, whooping, hollering, and firing off more shots.

The team bolted, heading off the road into a meadow.

Willy Jo pulled up hard on the reins. "Whoa, Jenny! Whoa, Jim!"

The pair paid no heed, careening this way and that, nearly upsetting the buggy with every turn.

"Jenny! Jim! Whoa!" he hollered louder, using all his might to pull back.

The team finally rolled to a halt in the middle of the field.

Willy Jo shook his fist in the darkness. "Crazy rider!"

Beside him on the seat, his mother gasped breathlessly. "Scared the life out of me!"

Vanda Mae pointed toward the road. "Look!"

A carriage had pulled off, heading toward them. He recognized Eck Danvers' voice before he could see his face in the pale lamplight.

"Young Winthrop! Didn't expect to see you here."

The surprise in his voice seemed forced, insincere.

"Some mad man with a shotgun just ran us off the road. You see him?"

Danvers shook his head. "Heard shots. Didn't see noth—anything."

Vanda Mae spoke up from the back. "Mr. Danvers, have you seen April, my Morgan? She went missing tonight while we were at a trolley party in Salem."

"Missing, eh?" Again, his bewilderment sounded overdone. "Haven't seen hide nor hair of your Morgan since the day I rode her at your place." Touching the brim of his hat, he said, "Drive careful, now."

When he'd pulled away, Virginia said, "I don't believe I ever met that gentleman, but the name Danvers . . . where do I know that from?"

Reluctant to explain, Willy Jo was relieved when Vanda Mae offered an answer. "He's the one who put Willy Jo and his daddy at odds over my Morgan."

"I see," Virginia said coolly.

Pulling onto the road, Willy Jo couldn't shake the feeling that Danvers knew a lot more than he'd let on, perhaps even the whereabouts of April. But how could Willy Jo ever find out?

~~~

When Vanda Mae arrived home and went into the library with Willy Jo to tell her daddy that April was missing, he accepted the news with equanimity as she had expected. But the following morning at the breakfast table, when she said she was going to Steadmans' with Bobby Dan, she wasn't prepared for his reaction.

"You must *promise* you'll stay off that horse from Saratoga."

She glared at Willy Jo.

"No reason to give him the evil eye," her daddy scolded. "Just about every customer who's come to the lumber yard this week has told tales about that filly. Now promise me you'll stay off her, or you'll stay home."

Unwilling to lie, but even more unwilling to stay behind, Vanda Mae mumbled, "I promise."

CHAPTER 7

Vanda Mae struggled with herself all morning long, caught between wanting to cancel plans to go riding at the Steadmans', and her curiosity to see the race horse even if she couldn't get on its back. Her mind seemed to vacillate with every basketful of manure she cleaned from the stable floor, every bucket of corn and oats she dumped into the manger, every stroke of the brush as she groomed Hurricane. At two o'clock, when Bobby Dan came to fetch her, she made no mention of her promise not to ride the race horse from Saratoga. And at the Steadmans', the moment Porky led the filly from the stable, the promise fled from her mind.

Lightning was a dark, dappled gray—a steely color unlike other thoroughbreds of Vanda Mae's acquaintance, which had all been some version of brown. The horse's head and neck had an elegant, long look that was carried out by the proportions of her body and legs. Even her tail was pretty, not thin and shabby like some retired racers.

From the first moment Vanda Mae patted the filly's shoulder she felt as if they belonged together. Lightning nickered and bobbed her head up and down, then she nuzzled Vanda Mae's neck and tried to stick her nose into the pocket of her breeches.

Porky, who had the build of a fighter and the congeniality of Santa Clause, laughed. "She didn't warm up to me nearly that fast. What's your secret, Vanda Mae? Got sugar lumps in your pocket?"

She pushed Lightning's nose away from her breeches then stroked her cheek. "I don't have a thing for her except a gentle touch and soft words. I hope she'll let me get on her now that we've made an acquaintance."

Keeping a tight grip on her lead rein, Porky said, "I'll hold her steady, 'less she decides to buck or rear. Then, you're on your own."

Bobby Dan gave Vanda Mae a hand up. She slid into the saddle as gently as possible, keeping up a soothing patter. "Good girl. Steady now, girl. You're doing fine. You and I are going to be good friends, aren't we?"

Lightning remained calm while Bobby Dan adjusted her stirrups. Porky said, "I'll walk you 'round some, case she forgets her manners." He started to make a small circle in a counter-clockwise direction around the meadow—the direction the horse was accustomed to traveling from her racing days.

Vanda Mae continued to pat her neck and praise her. "Good girl, Lightning. You're doing fine. You just take me on a nice, slow tour of your pasture."

When they had returned to the starting point, Porky asked, "Want to try her alone now?"

Vanda Mae consulted Lightning. "What do you think, girl? Can you behave yourself if Porky lets go?"

She nickered contentedly.

"Lightning seems to favor the idea," said Porky.

Vanda Mae grinned. "You can leave us on our own."

He patted Lightning on the neck. "Mind your p's and q's. Don't want Vanda Mae coming off your back 'fore she's ready." He unclasped the lead rein.

Vanda Mae said a silent prayer then gave a gentle nudge with her knees. "Lightning, walk."

The horse immediately obeyed. Vanda Mae tried a wider circle this time, praying Lightning would do as she asked, and wouldn't sense her apprehension. Keeping up a constant patter of praise, they soon returned to the others.

Porky patted Lightning's neck. "Good girl. That's the best you've ever done." To Vanda Mae, he said, "Better let me unsaddle her. Then we can go for a ride on horses we trust."

Without even thinking, Vanda Mae told him, "I'd like to work with Lightning a little longer, if you don't mind. I want to try her at a trot."

Porky hesitated. "She might take off."

"I'll keep a tight grip."

Bobby Dan told Porky, "If you and I ride just ahead of Vanda Mae on either side, Lightning's more likely to behave."

The fellows mounted their horses and preceded Vanda Mae around the pasture. They made several circles, then a figure eight pattern. Twenty minutes later, Lightning had shown no sign of wanting to break into a canter.

Porky pulled up in front of the stable. "That's enough for one day."

Confident on Lightning and unwilling to dismount, Vanda Mae said, "Let's ride the trail through the woods. It's impossible to do more than trot there. Lightning will be fine, I'm sure of it!"

Porky shook his head. "Had her in the woods the other day. Spooked at everything except the cicadas!"

Bobby Dan said, "She'll never make a good saddle horse if you don't give her a chance to get used to the trail. Vanda Mae seems to have a real way with her."

Porky sighed. "All right, but we're coming back the second there's any trouble."

He led the way off his daddy's farm into the adjoining woods. Vanda Mae rode at the rear. At times, she thought she heard someone behind her, but each time she turned to look, she found nothing.

Lightning behaved like a perfect lady. Two or three miles later, they arrived at an open field and crossed it three abreast at a walk.

In the distance, dogs barked. Lightning's ears twitched. Beneath her, Vanda Mae felt the horse tense up. Suddenly, Lightning laid her ears back and took off.

Vanda Mae's heart raced. She pulled back on the reins with all her strength.

"Whoa, Lightning! Stop!"

The thoroughbred ignored her.

Again, she cried, "Whoa, girl! Whoa!"

Lightning galloped on.

Vanda Mae checked hard, jerking the reins sharply.

The horse paid no heed.

Desperate, Vanda Mae see-sawed the reins.

Lightning continued her charge—straight for a split rail fence!

Vanda Mae's grip tightened. This horse had no training to jump the fence. Surely she would balk and Vanda Mae would go flying over the rail the same way Rosalie had been thrown from Hurricane years ago.

Vanda Mae squeezed her eyes shut and prayed, *Lord, save me!*

CHAPTER 8

Alone in her room after returning from the Steadmans', Vanda Mae unbuttoned her shirt and studied her
right shoulder in the cheval glass. A bruise was already
beginning to show and the joint had begun to swell. At
least it wasn't crushed the way Rosalie's had been. The
pain was almost enough to make her cry. She told herself
it would feel better once Shani brought the ice pack
she'd asked for on her way up to her room.

She buttoned her shirt, sat on the window seat, and
looked out at the huge oak in the front yard. As she
watched squirrels chase one another across the branches
she wondered how she'd keep her injury a secret when
every move of her right arm hurt from her shoulder blade
to her fingertips. It had been too painful to even pull her
self onto Hurricane's saddle. Porky and Bobby Dan
together had boosted her up so she could ride home.

Gaspar had given her a curious look when she'd
asked him to unsaddle and groom her horse rather than
doing it herself, but he hadn't asked questions. And her
mother, who would have been full of curiosity about the

afternoon outing and would have known intuitively that something was wrong, had already gone to her room to dress for dinner before Vanda Mae came in. Now, her daddy's carriage was rolling up the drive. Soon, she'd have to face him with the truth. And what acceptable reason could she give for breaking her word? *None!* He got out and came in through the front door carrying a package from the butcher shop beneath his arm while Willy Jo drove the buggy around back.

Willy Jo. She dreaded telling him what she'd done more than telling her father. The prospect gave her a headache. One wrong led to another and it had all started when she'd broken her promise by riding Lightning.

A knock sounded and Shani entered with the cold pack. "Hope you be feelin' better in time for dinner, Miss Vanda. I be puttin' steaks on the griddle in an hour—nice, thick filets your daddy just brought home." She turned to leave.

"Shani, wait." Vanda Mae pressed the ice pack to her shoulder. "I don't feel well enough to come down for dinner tonight. Could you please bring it up?"

Shani sighed. "I s'pose."

Vanda Mae's joint was so tender it was hard to say whether the pressure of the ice pack was worth the small amount of relief it brought. A few minutes later she pulled back the chenille spread on her canopy bed and lay down on her left side plumping pillows in such a manner as to keep the ice pack in place. She prayed for God's forgiveness, asked for his healing, and repeated several Bible verses from memory in an effort to ignore the pain.

A gentle knock and her mother's voice sounded at the door.

"May I come in, honey?"

"Yes, come in."

Mama set a letter she was holding on the bed stand and gave Vanda Mae a good looking over. "Shani said you asked for an ice pack. What happened?"

Vanda Mae sighed. "I rode the horse from Saratoga and fell off."

She drew a sharp breath.

Vanda Mae hurried to explain. "Everything was fine. Then, all of a sudden, she took off! Went straight toward a fence. When she swerved, I hit a fence rail like a sack of yams."

Mama sat on the edge of her bed, removed the ice pack, and unbuttoned Vanda Mae's shirt far enough to reveal her shoulder, more swollen and bruised than before, despite the cold pack.

Mama stood. "I'm ringing up the doctor."

She was nearly to the door when Vanda Mae protested. "I'm only bruised. I don't need a doctor!"

Her mother's voice grew panicky. "How can you know? You might end up with a shoulder that doesn't work anymore, just like Rosalie!"

"Mama, wait!" Vanda Mae cried, but her mother was already out the door and on her way downstairs to the phone.

A moment later she heard her father's footsteps in the hall and called to him. "Daddy, would you come here, please?" The instant he crossed her threshold, her guilt increased ten-fold. He appeared refreshed and relaxed from his bath and was almost smiling until his gaze fell on her shoulder.

His brows furrowed and he was clearly on the brink of a question when she spoke again. "I disobeyed you, Daddy. I rode Steadmans' race horse and . . ." Her throat clogging with shame, she forced out the next words. "I fell off. I'm sorry."

His distress, apparent in both his silence and his scowl, brought her to tears that leaked out, running across her nose. He offered her his handkerchief, his expression softening as he pulled up a chair to sit and face her. "I'm sorry, darlin'. Sorry you got hurt, and sorry you broke your promise."

She sobbed quietly. When her crying was in check she looked again into her daddy's face, now pensive.

He spoke softly. "I suppose what's bothering me as much as anything is wondering how honest you'd have been if you hadn't gotten hurt today. Would you ever have told me that you'd disobeyed?"

She closed her eyes letting her silence and more tears answer for her.

He brushed his hand across her damp cheek. "Vanda, honey, look at me."

She choked back her sobs, regaining fragile control as she focused on his soft brown eyes.

"I love you, darlin', but I'm going to have to punish you. You know that, don't you?"

She nodded against the pillowcase.

"Your mother and I will talk it over and decide what's fair."

Her throat was too tight to reply. More tears leaked out.

He bent and kissed her on the head, then turned to go, pausing to tap his finger against the letter her mother had left on the bed stand. "Here's news from your sister. It'll surprise you."

Her mother returned a minute later to say the doctor would arrive in about an hour. She managed to get into the tub for a bath and eat a few bites of the filet Shani brought despite constant pain. When the woman had taken away the dinner tray and supplied her with a fresh ice pack, Vanda Mae reached for the letter from Rosalie.

She was indeed surprised to learn that her sister had moved to a new address and that their aunt and uncle were no longer keeping shop. But she had little time to ponder the news, for the doctor arrived the moment after she had finished reading the letter.

Upon a careful—and painful—examination of her shoulder, he was able to convince her parents that no bones were broken and that she was *not* crippled for life like Rosalie. He predicted that in two weeks she would be over the worst of it, and eventually she would be completely mended. In the meanwhile, she could ease her pain with cold packs and the pills in the tiny bottle he left on her bed stand.

Through her open door floated the voices of her parents in conference with the doctor in the hallway but she couldn't make out the words. Minutes later, her folks came back into her room. Her daddy spoke first.

"Your mama and I have discussed your punishment and come to a decision."

Her mother said, "You're confined to your room. Tomorrow, you're to start packing your trunk. You and I are going north to visit Rosalie and your aunt and uncle. We'll stay in Michigan until month's end."

Michigan! The thought of leaving Tanglewood compounded her misery—no more evening outings on horseback with Willy Jo and her daddy. She wouldn't even be able to watch Jewel grow. But she dared not complain.

Her father must have read her thoughts. "I know it'll be hard on you, but maybe next time you'll consider the consequences before breaking a promise."

~~~

They had been gone the better part of an hour when she heard Willy Jo's footsteps in the hall. Moments later he stood in her open doorway, his expression sober.

She made a vain attempt to smile. "Come on in."

Accepting her invitation, he repositioned the chair by her bedside, straddling it to lean his arms across the back.

Vanda Mae didn't need words to know what Willy Jo must be thinking. Nor did she wish to broach the subject of her fall while he was looking so cross. She avoided the topic by posing a question. "Did you ride down by the river tonight?"

He shook his head. "Didn't feel up to it." Again, he grew silent. His scowl lines deepened.

Vanda Mae grew contrite. "I really made a mess of things. I should have listened to you."

He grumbled.

A quiet moment lapsed—a moment in which Vanda Mae could well imagine the angry thoughts running through Willy Jo's mind. He rose from his chair and started to leave.

"Willy Jo, wait!"

He paused, regarding her over his shoulder.

"Mama and I are going to visit Rosalie. Did you know?"

He nodded. "Give your sister my greetings."

"Promise you'll exercise Hurricane for me while I'm away."

He turned to face her again, his expression one of incredulity.

"*Please*, Willy Jo. You don't have April to ride anymore, and Hurricane will miss his outings terribly."

After a moment's thought, he mumbled, "I can't promise." Then he disappeared.

~~~

Willy Jo's stomach soured as he cinched Hurricane's saddle in place and started for home. He cared not a whit that his daddy had banned him from the family farm. His quarrel now was with Bobby Dan, the spoiled, selfish, shortsighted younger brother who cared for no one and nothing but himself, and had caused all manner of hurt in the process.

As Hurricane trotted along the dark driveway, Willy Jo barely noticed the oppressive night air too moist to dry the perspiration on his brow, or the musty essence of the piney woods. A concert of cicadas and crickets filled the night with a relentless rhapsody, but they played only a quiet accompaniment to the loud, heated words buzzing in Willy Jo's head.

Light spilled from the open door of his father's stable as he approached. Inside, Bobby Dan was practicing handsprings down the center aisle. Quietly, Willy Jo slid off Hurricane's back, stepping inside to confront Bobby Dan as he sprang his way toward him.

Abruptly, the favored son halted, instantly trading a momentary look of surprise for a smile that couldn't completely hide his apprehension.

"Willy Jo, what brings you home?"

"Why'd you do it?" he demanded in a low, bitter tone.

Bobby Dan put on a mask of innocence. "Do what, big brother?"

Willy Jo shoved him hard. "Why'd you let Vannie-Mae get on that horse?"

Bobby Dan backed away. "She insisted! You know as well as I do, you can't tell that girl anything where horses are—"

Willy Jo pushed him so hard, he fell. "I've half a mind to hurt your shoulder the way you did Vannie-Mae's!"

His brother scrambled backward across the dirt floor of the stable. "This isn't about horses, is it? You're sweet on her!"

Willy Jo pursued, tempted to plant the toe of his boot in his brother's midsection.

Before he could act on the urge, his daddy's voice boomed forth from the doorway behind him. "Willy Jo! Leave him be!"

He turned to face the man.

Cheeks scarlet, eyes flashing, his father came toward him. "You've got no place here! Now, get out!"

Willy Jo stood firm. "Not till I've settled my differences with Bobby Dan."

Willy Jo's daddy shoved him forcefully toward the door. "Is this the way I taught ya to get along with your little brother?"

Sparks ignited within. Willy Jo drew up a fist and planted it in his daddy's gut.

He doubled over, windless.

Willy Jo towered over his daddy for the first time in his life. "Bobby Dan's your favorite. That's what you taught me about my little brother!" He turned to Bobby Dan, yanking him up off the floor by the front of his shirt. "You may have Daddy fooled, but you don't fool me. You're nothing but a spoiled brat without a farming bone in your body. The sooner you make Daddy understand that, the better!" He tossed him down again.

Thoughts racing, Willy Jo hurried outside and leaped onto Hurricane's back, digging his heels into the gelding's flanks. Beneath a starless, moonless sky, he galloped off, the rumble of thunder at Hurricane's tail.

CHAPTER 9

Michigan

On Wednesday, Vanda Mae arrived in Michigan with Mama to a warm welcome by her sister, Rosalie, her sister's friend, Kenton, and her Aunt Lottie, and Uncle Ben. Rosalie helped her unpack in the bedroom they would share. On the ride from the train depot, Vanda Mae had explained how her favorite horse had been stolen on Friday night when Willy Jo had ridden it to Salem, and how she'd hurt her shoulder the following afternoon, thus causing her father's hasty plans to send her and Mama to Traverse City. Now, Rosalie was eager for other news.

"Aside from Daddy being terribly disappointed about your horse and your accident, how is he?"

Vanda Mae paused as she placed her underthings in the drawer Rosalie had cleared for her. "Daddy's fine—at least as far as his health is concerned, but he's been cross as a bear with two cubs and a sore toe since he heard the news Gaspar gave him Sunday morning."

Having hung one of Vanda Mae's dresses in the closet, Rosalie turned to face her. "The only way Gaspar could displease Daddy is if there's something wrong with his driving horses. Did one of them take sick?"

Vanda Mae shook her head. "Worse. They were both missing from the south pasture that morning. There weren't any holes in the fence, either. They just vanished without a trace!"

A few quiet moments lapsed while Rosalie rearranged hat boxes on her closet shelf to make room. Vanda Mae tried to help, but in her injured state, her assistance caused more problems than it solved.

Laughing at her own ineptitude, Vanda Mae said, "I'm just going to get out of your way and let you arrange things. You're far more practiced using your left hand than I shall ever be."

She had started to back out of the closet when she paused to inspect a pair of ladies' knickerbockers hanging on the rod. "I've never known you to own a pair of these. Have you taken up cycling since you came north?"

"No. I . . . uh . . . Mr. McCune bought those for me thinking it would help me gather the courage to . . ."

"To ride tandem with him? What a romantic notion, touring the city on a bicycle built for two. Of course, balancing will be—"

"The knickerbockers aren't intended for the purpose of cycling," Rosalie said as she shooed Vanda Mae out of her way.

Vanda Mae remained planted, her hand on her hip. "What then?"

Rosalie's cheeks reddened. "If you must know, I'm considering getting on a horse again."

"Rosalie!" Vanda Mae broke into a wide smile.

"Mr. McCune wanted to buy me a fancy, expensive riding habit but I told him that might be a complete waste, if I never actually put my foot into a stirrup."

Leading Rosalie away from the closet to a straight-backed chair, Vanda Mae pulled up another one for herself. "Sit down this minute and tell me how Mr. McCune managed to revive your interest in horseback riding."

Rosalie sat and shared the story of Susan Reddick, a young friend of Mr. McCune's, finishing with, "I know you'd like her. Perhaps Mr. McCune will take us all to the Reddick place soon, so you two can meet."

Vanda Mae scowled.

"Now, you've got a face like a mule eating briars," Rosalie gently scolded.

With a sigh, Vanda Mae explained. "As punishment for riding the Steadmans' racing horse when I promised not to, Daddy has forbid me to get on a horse again for a month." She paused to put on a smile. "But I want to meet Susan and her daddy and see their horses, and I surely want to be there when you ride again."

"Don't get your heart set on my doing it anytime soon. I'm about a ton short on courage."

Vanda Mae winked. "Then I'm going to start praying for that ton to be delivered post haste."

Rosalie reached for Vanda Mae's hand, giving it a squeeze. "Tell me, how is Bobby Dan?"

Vanda Mae gazed heavenward.

Rosalie smiled. "You know what I mean, other than the usual handsprings, cartwheels, and crazy antics he's always pulling."

Vanda Mae sighed. "He pulled the biggest antic of them all three days ago."

"I hope he didn't hurt himself doing acrobatics."

Moving to the fainting couch, Vanda Mae leaned back. "I'll tell you what happened." She relayed Willy Jo's description of the spat concerning himself, Bobby Dan, and his father. "So Bobby Dan up and ran away from home the very next night, and nobody knows where he's gone. Of course, Mrs. Winthrop is beside herself, and Willy Jo is taking it real hard, giving himself all the blame. In my opinion, it's their daddy who's at fault. He ought to know his chances of making a farmer out of Bobby Dan are about as good as sneaking dawn past a rooster."

"Maybe he'll see that, now that both sons are away from home." Rosalie got up and put Vanda Mae's gloves in her top drawer, then she turned to face her. "I don't suppose Willy Jo sent any greetings for me—I mean, with all that was happening, it probably didn't cross his mind."

"Willy Jo *did* send his greetings."

Rosalie's brow wrinkled.

"He said, 'Give your sister my greetings.' That was his precise message."

Rosalie released a quiet sigh.

Vanda Mae pressed on. "Now tell me about this Mr. McCune. In your letters, you said he's a friend, but I think there's more to it than that."

Rosalie closed the bedroom door and began a long description of her association with Mr. McCune that included the day he kept her from running away, their current efforts to help Aunt Lottie and Uncle Ben regain ownership of their store, and all the events in between.

~~~

Although Aunt Lottie and Uncle Benjamin had been required to report for a half day's work at the candy factory early the following Saturday morning, Vanda Mae was enjoying a later, unhurried meal with Mr. McCune, her mother, and sister. Vanda Mae and Mama had devoted the previous two mornings to making acquaintance with the Doyle sisters, the next door neighbors, while Rosalie assisted Mr. McCune in his law office.

A conversation ensued about the difficulties of restoring the candy shop to its rightful owners and the seemingly dead end that had been reached, concluding with Vanda Mae's question to her sister.

"What are you going to do next?"

Rosalie shrugged and turned to Mr. McCune. "Yes, what *are* we going to do next?"

After a moment's thought, a smile crept over his face. "We're going to forget about the problem and take that ride out to the Reddicks' just like we promised Susan when we rang her up last night. I could do with a few hours in the country on a good riding horse."

Mama smiled. "And I, the same." To Rosalie, she said, "No offense, dear, but after one day of euchre with Miss Ava and Miss Eda, and another day walking all about this fair city, I'm ready to climb aboard a good horse and ride."

To Rosalie, Vanda Mae said, "Be sure to put your knickerbockers on beneath your skirt before we go. You never know when that ton of courage might come tumbling down on you."

Rosalie set her napkin aside. "I'll wear them, but don't get your hopes up. That ton of courage you've been praying for seems to be on an ounce-at-a-time delivery schedule."

~~~

On the drive to the Reddicks', Vanda Mae spoke encouragingly of Rosalie riding again, as did Mama, but Rosalie showed no enthusiasm. The moment Mr. McCune brought his carriage to a halt in the driveway, Susan and her father welcomed them. With introductions accomplished, Mr. Reddick led them toward the stable, his comments directed at Rosalie.

"Susan has taken the liberty of saddling up Penny for you."

"She's so tall, it'll be easiest to use the mounting platform to get on her." Susan indicated a wooden structure near the end of the building. "But Daddy and I will be right there to steady her and adjust your stirrups once you're in the saddle."

Inside the stable, Penny was cross tied in the aisle, all brushed, bridled, and saddled as had been promised.

The moment Rosalie saw her, she took a step back. "I . . . I've changed my mind about riding today. Maybe some other time." She started to move away, but Vanda Mae prevented her, slipping her arm about her waist.

"I'm not going to let you run away this time, Sis. Penny is the perfect horse for you, I can tell just by looking at her. And you're going to get on her."

Mama stroked Penny's neck, giving her tack a cursory inspection. "Vanda Mae's right, Rosalie, Penny's a good choice, and getting on her will be easy as shoofly pie. You'll see."

John began unfastening the animal. "Like Susan said, we'll be right beside you every second. There's nothin' to worry about."

The mounting platform was situated beneath the shade of an oak. With a tight grip, Vanda Mae led Rosalie up the stairs. "It's just one little step from here, Sis."

Mama smiled up at them. "There's no better time than now, to get on a horse again, dear."

"You can do it, Miss Foxe, just like I did," said Susan.

Rosalie stood staring at the saddle for what seemed like an eternity.

"Don't keep the Reddicks and poor Penny waiting forever, dear," said Mama. "Just say a little prayer and lower yourself onto the saddle."

Rosalie stiffened, her back ramrod straight.

Kenton took Mama by the elbow. "Mrs. Foxe, perhaps Rosalie will do better with fewer people looking on. Come, let me show you my pride and joy, my horse, Judge."

As he led her off toward the stable, she called over her shoulder, "You can do it, dear, I know you can!"

With Mama gone, Vanda Mae prayed quietly. "Lord, please give Rosalie the fortitude to bend down, reach for the saddle horn, and settle herself on Penny. Amen."

Slowly, Rosalie bent toward the horse.

CHAPTER 10

North Carolina

Full from the catfish dinner Shani had served this Friday night, Willy Jo leaned back on the grassy cushion of the riverbank, pulled his cap down over his eyes, and inhaled deeply of the magnolia essence before expelling it with a sigh. While locusts droned their tedious tunes, he pondered his circumstances since Vanda Mae's accident.

Thirteen days had lapsed—thirteen evenings since she'd gone riding with him. And nine days had passed since he'd heard her voice or seen her face. Tanglewood wasn't the same without her.

Now, at the end of his sixth week at Foxe Brothers, he couldn't help wondering if or when he would get back to the farm chores he loved. He'd prayed God would forgive him for the fight with his brother and father, but he hadn't been able to bring himself to go to his daddy and apologize. Bobby Dan had departed suddenly and mysteriously. Certainly Daddy needed help. Willy Jo had hoped his father would ask him to lend a hand, then he'd be able to say he was sorry, but it was a foolish thought.

He recalled the fact that Mr. Foxe had spoken with his daddy just two days ago, and the exact words. *Your daddy is claiming you're all to blame for Bobby Dan leaving home. When I told him it was just as much his fault for trying to force the boy into farming, he raised more fuss than a weasel in a hen house and told me to mind my own business. Guess you'll be staying on here awhile, son.*

The mere recollection made Willy Jo smolder within. Getting to his feet, he mounted Hurricane, walked him out of the woods, then dug his heels into his belly, racing as fast as he could across the pasture. When he slowed to a walk to cool the horse down, he realized he couldn't outrun anger or frustration, but perhaps with God's help he could find a way to put it behind him. He prayed it would be so.

When he had unsaddled Hurricane, fed him a ration of oats, and turned him out to pasture, he walked back to the house. Shani was working in the kitchen, and greeted him as he removed his boots in the back room.

"Mr. Foxe said to tell ya he done turned in for the night. Is there anything I can get ya 'fore I do the same?"

"No, thank you, Shani. I'm going up and take my bath soon."

She wiped her hands on her apron. "I'll go on up and draw the water for ya."

"No need. I'll draw my own bath," Willy Jo told her, intending to sit in the library and read the paper for a spell. But when he walked into the room, he found an open letter atop the newspaper on the table between Mr. Foxe's chair and his. He remembered then that a letter from up north had been waiting for Mr. Foxe on the table in the front hall when they'd arrived home, but he'd saved it for later knowing Shani was ready to put dinner on the table. He evidently intended for Willy Jo to read it, too. He recognized Vanda Mae's hand at the top of the page.

Dearest Daddy,

How I wish you had been here today! Mr. McCune, the lawyer friend of Uncle Benjamin and Aunt Lottie, took Mama, Rosalie, and me to a horse farm and Rosalie actually sat on the back of a horse! She only stayed there a minute or two, and wouldn't let Mr. Reddick—he's the man who owns the farm—lead the horse around at all, but at least she made a start at getting over her fear.

Daddy, I know I'm not supposed to ride a horse while I'm here, but I hope you'll reconsider. My shoulder is much better than it was, and in one more week, I'm sure it will be good as new. If you would let me ride at the Reddicks', I think I can convince Rosalie to ride along beside me with our horses at a walk. Please give me your permission. Mama absolutely will not allow me to mount a horse without your blessing.

I must end here and let Mama write the rest of our news. Give my greetings to Willy Jo if he is still with you at Tangle-wood, or when you see him next, if he is not.

Your dutiful daughter, Vanda Mae.

Dearest Fergus,

As Vanda Mae has informed you, Rosalie is progressing toward the day when she will once again ride horseback! Please let us hear from you soon regarding Vanda Mae's re-quest to ride beside her sister. She may well be able to give Rosalie the extra measure of confidence she so sorely needs to take the next step.

*As for other news, our stay here has been very pleasant—
and interesting. Mr. McCune has enlisted Rosalie's help in
untangling the problems that put my sister and brother out of
their shop. I don't know if they'll ever succeed at getting to the
bottom of the mess, but Rosalie and Mr. McCune seem to be
making an excellent success of their friendship. In fact, Rosalie has already hinted that she might like to stay on up north
past summer's end and I wouldn't be at all opposed, should it
come to that.*

*Is Willy Jo still with you? I pray he has made amends with
his kin and moved back home. Virginia would take great sol-
ace in his return, especially since the disappearance of Bobby
Dan. Did he come back home yet? By the time this reaches
you, perhaps my prayers for both boys will have been answered and the wayward sons will have returned. I'm eager to
know if Winthrops have had cause to celebrate a family reunion.*

*I must close now and put this in the mail. I miss you, my
darling, and pray the August heat hasn't been too hard on
you. The climate is very pleasant here by the big lake, but after all my years in Old North State, I find I miss the mountains
at Blowing Rock. Perhaps we can take a holiday together
there this fall, when Vanda Mae has returned to the Academy
and family and business matters are less pressing.*

Your loving wife, Minnie.

Willy Jo read the portions about Rosalie a second time before setting the letter down. A strange sense of relief came
over him that, despite the longtime assumption he and Rosalie
would someday marry, she was now enjoying the friendship of
another man, freeing him of guilt over his attraction to her

younger sister. But relief was not the only emotion deep within his heart right now. An emptiness had set in, and a longing for as much love in his own family as he sensed among the Foxes.

Needing to ponder these thoughts and more, he wandered out to the pasture, soon riding bareback atop Hurricane whom he walked along the road toward his daddy's place. As dusk set in and whippoorwills soared overhead making their plaintive pleas, he longed to turn up the drive toward home, but instead, he kept to the road, passing his father's largest cornfield. Even in the dim light he could see that the stalks were not as high as they should be this time of year. Weeds were encroaching on some of the rows he'd helped cultivate and plant during spring recess from school, but other rows had been recently hoed.

Arriving at the path to the hog pen and barn, he turned up the two-track trail. Off to the side stood his daddy's wagon, one wheel missing. He wondered why Lincoln hadn't fixed it. Daddy never left equipment in disrepair, but always put Lincoln, his trusted farm hand with wheelwright and blacksmith skills, right to the task.

He continued on, toward the hog pens. Even from a distance he could hear the anguished roars and moans of hungry pigs. Drawing nearer, he saw that the trough in the pen of feeder pigs was empty and their wallow dry. He dismounted, tethered Hurricane, and went into the barn in search of feed. A basket stood beneath the chute of the potato cleaner, half-full. Willy Jo cranked the handle, sending more cleaned potatoes down the chute until the basket could hold no more, then he carried it out and dumped it in the trough. The pigs grunted and squealed in their rush to feed. Making more trips to the barn, Willy Jo fetched basket after basket of corn until the trough was full.

As he stood back to watch the hogs feed, he noticed that some of the animals were maturing well, but others were downright scrawny. He wished he'd been there to make sure they were *all* receiving sufficient feed. Surely each and every hog would have prospered under his care. As it was, several of them needed considerable fattening up to attain a normal weight for their age.

On his way back to the barn, he paused at the sty of the sow who'd been lame at the start of July. At least now, she appeared to be moving normally on all fours.

In the barn once more, he gathered water buckets in hand, headed for the well, then carried several gallons of water to the wallow until it was thoroughly muddy again. Leaning his foot on the fence rail, he watched as the satiated pigs rolled in the cool, wet earth, acquiring a muddy coat of protection against flies, mosquitoes, and parasites. Their satisfied grunts were music to his ears, but why hadn't his father properly tended the hogs himself?

With a heavy heart he mounted Hurricane and continued on, taking a hard clay path toward the hired man's house. Maybe Lincoln could tell him why the wagon had gone unrepaired, the cornfield wasn't hoed, and some hogs were underfed. Several yards from the house he heard a man's voice, song-like. The sound grew louder and bawdier as he moved closer. The words and tune were unrecognizable, but the voice was easily identified, as was the state of its owner. Lincoln was obviously in a bad way, the victim of too much whiskey.

Now, Willy Jo knew why the cornfield was neglected, the hogs underfed, and the wagon in disrepair. Lincoln had lapsed into his old, bad habit, one he had overcome years ago, but had evidently taken up again. Without Lincoln's help, or that of either son, there was only so much Willy Jo's daddy could do.

Sympathy battled with resentment in Willy Jo's heart. He hated seeing the family farm in decline. He hated more his father's stubbornness that kept the two of them apart. Swinging Hurricane around, he trotted down the clay path onto the road and nudged the horse's flanks with his heels, setting him into a canter toward Tanglewood.

CHAPTER 11

Michigan

"Don't forget these!" Vanda Mae reminded Rosalie, holding up the knickerbockers she'd worn to the Reddicks' one week ago.

With a sigh, Rosalie pulled the pant-like garment up beneath her skirt and stepped in front of the mirror. As she arranged the folds of blue serge over the knickerbockers, Vanda Mae came up behind her.

"You're going to do it today, Sis. You're going to ride Penny around the ring and nothing bad is going to happen."

Rosalie met Vanda Mae's gaze in the mirror. "I'd be a lot more sure of myself if you could ride beside me." When she turned to face Vanda Mae, worry lines creased her brow. "As it is, I'm so tied in knots, I'm not even sure I can manage to get in a saddle again."

"Oh, go on!" Vanda Mae offered a hug. She was releasing Rosalie when the sound of a buggy coming to a stop in front of the house caught their attention.

Vanda Mae hurried to the window and pushed back the curtain. "It's the Western Union hack." She headed for the door, returning moments later to place a telegram from Daddy in Rosalie's hands.

She focused on the missive and read. "'Permission granted to ride with Rosalie. Only. Letter to follow.'"

At her puzzled look, Vanda Mae quickly explained. "I wrote Daddy last week and told him you were considering riding again, and that I thought you'd be more likely to follow through if I could ride with you."

Rosalie drew a sharp breath. "Now, you've done it, Vanda Mae! Now you've really put me on the spot!"

Vanda Mae wagged her finger. "Only a few minutes ago you told me you'd be more sure of yourself if I could ride with you. Well, you got your wish. Nothing's going to stop you, now!" Going straight to her trunk, Vanda Mae pulled out the riding breeches and shirt she'd brought north just in case, but hadn't bothered to unpack.

Rosalie placed her hand over her stomach. "I've got a flock of butterflies in here, and they're starting to dance."

"We'll net them and all will go well. You'll see."

~~~

An hour later, as the carriage drew near the stable, Vanda Mae saw that Rosalie was gripping the seat so tightly, her fingers had turned white. She sent up a silent plea. *Dear Lord, send Rosalie courage, and send it now!*

Horses for Kenton and Mama were led from the stable, all saddled and ready. They mounted and rode off, then Rosalie and Mr. Reddick led Penny out of the stable while Vanda Mae and Susan followed atop chestnut mares.

As Rosalie drew near the wooden mounting platform, a lesson from the Bible came to Vanda Mae's mind. "Remember, Rosalie, you can do all things through Christ."

Rosalie gave a nod and began to mount the platform, then stalled beside the huge horse.

Vanda Mae couldn't let her stop now. "Do this for yourself, Rosalie. You can, if you *want* to!"

Rosalie winced and remained stiff as a mannequin.

Vanda Mae offered a prayer. "Dear Lord, my sister's a tad scared just now. Wrap her in a mantel of courage. Bind her fears and cast them out. Take her in your arms and set her on Penny's back, then carry her there until she knows no doubt or apprehension. In Jesus name, Amen."

Slowly, Rosalie lowered herself onto Penny's back, took up the reins, and relaxed into the gentle jostling of the saddle as Mr. Reddick led Penny around the riding ring.

Vanda Mae and Susan rode on either side, offering encouraging words every step of the way. Rosalie took a second trip around without Mr. Reddick's help. By the end of the hour, she was riding around the ring alone.

Practice continued another half hour until Mama and Mr. McCune returned, joyful to see Rosalie riding alone, and with considerable confidence. Mr. Reddick helped Rosalie to dismount, and everyone headed into the barn.

Vanda Mae turned to Mama and Mr. McCune. "Now that Rosalie is riding again, when can we come back? It would be best not to let too much time pass before Rosalie takes the saddle again."

Mr. Reddick, who was removing Penny's saddle, turned to Vanda Mae. "I'm taking Susan to Chicago, to a horse auction this week, but you're welcome to come out and ride next Sunday."

"Next Sunday, it is," said Mr. McCune.

CHAPTER 12

Willy Jo was thankful that Mr. Foxe had closed up shop and brought him home a couple of hours earlier than usual on this still, sultry, Saturday afternoon. In his spare time before dinner, he mounted Hurricane and headed for his daddy's farm, perspiration rolling down his face and dripping off his chin with each sluggish step of the grey gelding. But he gave little thought to the heat now, and was only slightly aware of the musty essence of the woods that shaded this stretch of road. Foremost on his mind were last night's images of neglect on his daddy's hog farm.

As Willy Jo rounded the bend, the woods gave way to a clearing. In the distance he could see his daddy laboring alone at the axle of his broken-down wagon, struggling to replace the wheel that had been missing the night before. In the shade of a nearby poplar stood his team, waiting to be hitched.

With a nudge of his heels, he urged Hurricane to trot. His father seemed unaware of his approach, grunting and straining as he toiled to position the heavy, iron-rimmed wheel on the axle. Willy Jo quickly dismounted and grabbed hold of the spokes, lending enough muscle power to mate the hub to the axle.

Daddy straightened and heaved a sigh. His hand on his back, he slipped off his straw hat and mopped his sweaty forehead on his rolled-up sleeve. With barely a glance at Willy Jo, he pulled the wide, fringed brim down over his eyes again, mumbling, "Didn't hear ya comin'."

Lacking a reply, Willy Jo began tightening down the wheel. Without so much as a word of thanks, his daddy went to fetch the team. Willy Jo waited while he backed them into position, then helped hitch them up, attaching the right tug to the wagon while his daddy secured the left.

When his daddy swung up onto the driver's seat, Willy Jo fought the urge to climb up beside him as he'd done hundreds of times since he'd been a small boy. Instead, he forced himself to walk away, toward Hurricane.

He was about to mount the horse when Daddy spoke up. "Tie that rascal to the wagon and ride up to the house with me. I'm sure Kezia has enough lemonade for us both."

The soft rhythm of the horses' hooves on the dusty roadbed, the quiet creaking of the wooden wagon wheels, the unremitting buzz of locusts in tree limbs high above the road proved a poor substitute for conversation. Nevertheless, Willy Jo was mighty thankful for the few sentences already spoken, and he searched his heart for appropriate words of his own. Sadly, he concluded that no matter what subject he might broach, he was sure to say the wrong thing. So he kept his silence all the way to the house, as did his daddy, speaking only words of thanks when Kezia brought cooling beverages to them both in their repose beneath the fronds of the huge willow in the dooryard.

Willy Jo didn't miss the look of keen interest in the dark-skinned housekeeper's eyes when she saw him, nor the way she pressed her lips together to keep from speaking out of turn. He was wondering why his mother hadn't come out to greet him when his daddy spoke again.

"Your mama's out to a sewin' circle meetin'. She'll be right sorry she missed ya."

"Give her my love," Willy Jo promptly replied, wishing affection for his father were as easily felt and expressed.

Their lemonade glasses were half-empty when his daddy saw fit to speak again. "Been a lot of horses stolen hereabouts this month. Two of Benders' came up missin' just last night." He named neighbors on a nearby farm. "I've been keepin' my roans tied up outside my bedroom window at night." He paused, then his gaze met Willy Jo's and he was certain the sore subject of April would come up. Instead, conversation took a new turn. "Heard from your brother the other day."

"How—"

Daddy hastened to explain. "Fool kid up and joined a travelin' show. He's doin' acrobatics at fairs up north—in Wisconsin last I heard."

Willy Jo was still absorbing the news when a grin bloomed on his daddy's face. "Should've known I'd never make a farmer out of him. At least he's happy."

At least he's happy. The sentiment rang in Willy Jo's head. Anger reared in his heart and words leaped off his tongue before he could stop them.

"All you care about is Bobby Dan! What about *me?* What about *my* happiness?"

His daddy's mouth fell open. Color invaded his cheeks. Willy Jo surged on.

"Bobby Dan never does wrong in your eyes. And I never do right! No matter how hard I try, I never hear a word of thanks or praise!" Tossing the remaining lemonade and ice from his glass, he plunked it down beside his father and sprang to his feet. "I wanted to come home. Goodness knows you need my help. I hoped things could be different between us, but I can see now, nothing's changed!"

He untied Hurricane and swung into the saddle.

"Willy Jo! Wait!"

Ignoring his father's plea, he set a course for Tangle- wood, putting the gelding into a canter despite the heat.

~~~

The full moon was a large, white treasure amidst a collection of lesser gems that shone through a hole in the clouds when Willy Jo gave up the notion of sleep, pulled on work pants and shirt, and ventured out of the manor house at midnight. The air was still heavy with moisture despite the passing of the thunderstorm that had moved through in the last hour. The continued heat and humidity, along with troubling thoughts of his latest encounter with his father, had kept him from finding entrance to dreamland.

Leaning against the fence, he gazed at the row of outdoor boxes alongside the stable. A restless Hurricane stood visible until clouds moved in to obscure stars and moon again. As warm winds breathed down his collar, he contemplated the hasty ending to his afternoon ride. He shouldn't have stormed off. He should have given his father a chance to talk. But pent-up anger, resentment, and yes, even jealousy, had destroyed the last fragment of tolerance he might have summoned for any words his daddy could have offered.

Without aforethought, he fetched Hurricane's bridle from the tack room, slipped them onto the horse, and mounted his bare back. Responding to some inner, magnetic force, he headed in the direction of his daddy's farm. There, following instinct rather than plan, he lit a lantern and tended the hog pen, carrying basket after basket filled with potatoes and corn.

Seeing a large abscess on one of the pigs, he removed the animal from the pen, then cleaned, lanced, and drained the infection. Afterward, he inspected the pen thoroughly, and by lantern light repaired a rough board that could have caused the break in the one animal's skin, allowing infection to set in.

From the barn, he fetched a hoe and basket, carried them along with an extra lantern to the nearby cornfield, and began digging weeds from between the stalks. Though he knew he couldn't hope to finish the work required in the field tonight, at least he could make a start, labor until fatigue overcame him, and return some other time. As he loosened the dirt, pulled out the grassy weeds, and laid them aside to collect later, he realized how much he'd missed putting his hands in the soil, turning the earth, cultivating the crop that was essential to a hog farmer's success —almost as much as he'd missed caring for the hogs. Down one long row and up another, he worked back and forth across the field until thunder rumbled. In the distance, lightning flashed. Another thunderstorm was moving in, making it unsafe to remain in the field. Quickly, he gathered uprooted weeds into his basket, took up his hoe, and headed for the barn where Hurricane was tethered, but uneasy.

The wind picked up, gusting in his face as they headed for Tanglewood. Rumblings of thunder made Hurricane shy and side-step.

"Get on, boy. It's all right," Willy Jo reassured him. "We'll be home soon, then you can hide in your box if you want."

Hurricane remained uneasy, so Willy Jo kept up a mindless, soothing patter until they reached the pasture gate where he dismounted to swing it open.

Lightning flashed.

Thunder boomed.

Hurricane bolted, ripping his reins free of Willy Jo's grip and taking off down the road as rain let loose.

"Whoa, boy! Come back!" Willy Jo shouted, running after him.

Another crack sounded—of gunfire, this time.

Then he heard Gaspar shout, "Stop, you thief!"

Before Willy Jo could identify himself, a second shot sent searing pain into his side. Clutching his wound, he slumped onto a hard, slippery bed of wet clay.

CHAPTER 13

As Rosalie dressed to spend a Sunday afternoon horseback riding at the Reddicks', Vanda Mae observed her carefully. "You look every bit a horsewoman, dressed in the new riding breeches and boots you bought from Millikens yesterday—except for the worry lines on your forehead."

Rosalie sighed. "I thought I had conquered my fears, but the butterflies are back."

"Maybe they'll settle soon. Say, did I tell you? When Susan rang us up last night to invite us over, she said her daddy bought a new mare at the Chicago auction."

"Only half a dozen times since last night."

"To hear Susan tell it, that new horse of hers is the finest mare this side of the Mason-Dixon line. I'd never say a word to disappoint her, but that mare can't be as nice as my April was."

"That's what you said last night," Rosalie reminded her.

Vanda Mae went on. "April was the finest riding horse I've ever seen. Daddy liked her so much, he—"

"—wanted to make her into a brood mare," Rosalie finished for her.

"I guess I told you that before, too."

Picking up her new riding gloves, Rosalie headed for the door. "If we don't get started soon, you'll have repeated your entire life's story before we get to the Reddicks', and it would be a pure shame to deprive Susan and her father the pleasure of hearing it." She grinned.

"At least I got your mind off the butterflies and made the creases in your forehead disappear." Vanda Mae smiled broadly.

A quarter of an hour later, Kenton pulled into the Reddicks' drive. Susan, who was in the ring riding a chestnut horse, headed toward Kenton's rig. As she drew closer, Vanda Mae said, "That horse Susan is on is the same color as April. Her blaze is like April's too, the way it flares out on the right side. And look at her legs. She's got three white socks exactly like April."

The moment the buggy came to a halt, Vanda Mae jumped out and ran to the horse. "April, it's you!" Vanda Mae's heart did somersaults.

The mare nickered and bobbed her head.

Vanda Mae reached for her bridle, stroking her nose, then hugging her neck. "I found you, girl! I can hardly believe it! I found you!"

April nuzzled Vanda Mae's neck and let out a soft whinney.

Susan backed the horse away with a firm command, then addressed Vanda Mae. "What are you talking about? This is Queenie, *my* horse, the one Papa bought for me at Chicago!"

"But she was stolen from me earlier this month!" Vanda Mae insisted.

"We have the papers to prove this horse is ours!" Susan claimed.

Rosalie, Kenton, Mama, and Susan's father joined Vanda Mae and Susan.

"Whoa, young ladies! What's this all about?" asked Susan's father.

With tears in her eyes, Susan turned to him. "Vanda Mae says Queenie is hers, that she was stolen, and we don't really own her. *Please* show her the paper that says we bought her, fair and square!"

Vanda Mae addressed her mother. "This is *April!* I'd know her anywhere! See the shape of her blaze, her three white socks, and the frost in her eyebrows?"

Mama took hold of April's bridle. She spoke softly to the animal, stroking her nose and inspecting her teeth and markings before turning to John. "My daughter's right, Mr. Reddick. My husband can prove this horse belongs to him, and she *was* stolen from us about three weeks ago."

John's expression hardened. "Then let your husband replevy the animal—put up security and take me to court." To Mr. McCune, he said, "You'll represent me in this matter, won't you?"

Mr. McCune seemed to look past him, at the stables in the distance, before focusing on his good friend. "I'm suffering from conflict of interest, being a family friend to both you and the Foxes. I'd be foolish to take either side in a dispute between you. But John, I'll give you this advice for free. If Mr. Foxe documents his ownership to the court's satisfaction, the animal will be returned to him."

Mama's gaze pinned Mr. Reddick. "And there's no doubt in my mind, you'll lose."

Kenton rested a hand on Mr. Reddick's shoulder. "From one friend to another, I believe your best recourse is to locate the fellow who brought the horse to auction."

Mr. Reddick gazed at April, then at Susan, his blue eyes clouding over.

His daughter brushed away a tear with the back of her riding glove. "Don't let them take Queenie, Papa! You said yourself, she's just the mare we need to build up our stock and keep the place going."

He reached up, caressing Susan's moist cheek. "We've got to do what's right."

"I won't give her up! I *won't!*" The young girl dug her heels into April's flanks and rode off in a cloud of dust.

Rosalie spoke up as the air cleared. "Mr. Reddick, I'll be glad to type up a letter from Mr. McCune to the auction house informing them that they've been party to traffic in stolen property and inquiring as to the seller's whereabouts. It might help you recover your investment so you can purchase some other animal."

"Something must be done to catch the thief, and the sooner, the better," said Mama.

A hand shading her eyes, Vanda Mae watched Susan and April disappear across a wide meadow and into the adjoining woods. "One thing's certain, I've just lost my hankering for a horseback ride. Maybe Mr. McCune should take us straight to his office so Rosalie can use his typing machine."

Mama nodded. "And we should wire my husband about April."

"I'd be much obliged for the help," said John, "but I don't think it'll make a difference. If the horse was stolen, the thief'd be long gone from Chicago by now."

"'Nothing venture, nothing win,' William Gilbert, *Iolanthe,* Act II," said Kenton. "If you'll fetch the address of the auction house and the papers on the horse, the Foxe ladies and I will post a letter before the day is through."

.

CHAPTER 14

Like the restless grey clouds in the sky above, Willy Jo couldn't suppress the uneasiness he was feeling as Mr. Foxe pulled onto the main road and turned toward his daddy's place to honor their invitation to Sunday dinner. A week ago, upon receiving a telephone message from Mr. Foxe that Willy Jo had suffered a gunshot wound, his daddy had come to pay him a visit. The injury was nothing serious, the bullet having only grazed his flesh, but the incident had brought about direct communication between them. For the first time in years, his daddy had seemed a mite sympathetic. For the first time in years, he hadn't jumped at a chance to condemn Willy Jo for the calamity that had befallen him. For the first time in years, Willy Jo had heard his father speak not one word about Bobby Dan.

But neither had his daddy thanked him for the help he'd given him with the wagon wheel, or the work done in the cornfield and the hog pen just before he was shot. The circumstances of the accidental shooting had been carefully explained. His daddy knew where he'd gone on Hurricane in the middle of the night, and why Gaspar had mistaken him for a horse thief on his return to Tanglewood. Even if his father had chosen to ignore the explanation, surely he couldn't ignore the hoed rows of corn, the full trough in the hog pen, and the repair he'd made. But no expression of gratitude had been forthcoming.

Perhaps Willy Jo was expecting too much. His father was slow to change. He should be thankful for the improvements he'd already seen. He tried to think less about his disappointment and more about the opportunity at hand.

As Mr. Foxe turned off the main road, the essence of phlox along his father's fence-lined drive filled the air. The perfume of the delicate flowers brought to mind his mother's sweet nature. He silently prayed that her gentle spirit would rule this day. And with the appearance of the sun through a rare hole in the grey heavens, hope sprang within that his petition was about to be answered. The sight of his daddy stepping out the door to greet him and Mr. Foxe with an equally rare smile seemed to confirm the fact.

"Fergus, Willy Jo, you're right on time. Kezia is ready to serve up." He rested his arm atop Willy Jo's shoulders as they went inside. Such displays of affection had been absent from their relationship since—Willy Jo couldn't remember when—and seemed unnatural now.

In the front hallway, he greeted his mother with his customary peck on the cheek. Her eyes were welling up, her voice a tad shaky when she greeted him.

"Good to see you, son."

He could only mumble a reply, his own throat growing tight as he cherished the familiar surroundings he'd missed for so long—the shadowbox of dried roses his mother had created years ago and hung on the foyer wall; her rose petit point chair cover when he seated her at the dining table; the polished oak sideboard his father had refinished when Willy Jo was still a boy in short pants. Now it was laden with the results of Kezia's culinary efforts. The sense of homecoming he'd experi-experienced each time he'd returned from a long stay at school, he would like to have known again, except now he felt like an outsider.

When they had settled around the table, his daddy offered his standard prayer. "Blessed be the Lord, and bountiful thy hand. For these, thy gifts, we give thee thanks. In Jesus name, Amen."

Kezia set before him half a clove-studded ham covered with pineapple rings. Despite the pretense of normalcy as it was carved and served along with her grits, yams, and sticky buns, tension flowed beneath the polite dinner table conversation. When the main course had come to an end and Kezia headed for the kitchen with a promise of cobbler made from home-grown peaches for dessert, a lull in the flow of words brought about a prompting from his mother.

"Jabe, you had something you wanted to ask Willy Jo today. Now's a good time."

Barely hiding his disquietude, his father focused on him. "Son," he paused as if the words he was about to say were not his own, "it's time ya moved back here—that is, if you're still of a mind to."

The invitation lacked conviction, and Willy Jo's first instinct was to refuse, but Mr. Foxe intervened with a smile that seemed unwarranted.

"I'll be hard put to replace Willy Jo at the lumber yard, Jabe, but I've been praying for weeks that this day would come." To Willy Jo, he said, "Of course, Tanglewood will be a mighty lonely place till my women come home from up north, but I'll have Gaspar help you move back home this very day."

Mama's eyes sparkled. "I'll be so thankful to have at least one of my boys under my roof again."

Daddy's mouth curved in a half-smile. "Then it's settled." With barely a pause, he continued on another subject.

As conversation continued between Daddy and Mr. Foxe, Willy Jo entertained private reservations about moving back into his father's house that bore a tart contrast to Kezia's sugary sweet cobbler.

~~~

Willy Jo was still considering his impending move home when he and Mr. Foxe arrived at Tanglewood. His troubled thoughts were interrupted when Shani came hurrying out the back door of the house, waving Mr. Foxe down as he headed toward the carriage barn.

"Mr. Fergus, Mr. Willy, wait up!" A smile stretched the limits of Shani's generous mouth as, huffing and puffing, she waddled up to the carriage and shoved an opened Western Union envelope into Mr. Foxe's hand. "Forgive me for . . . readin' your message, but . . . I had to know if it was news that could wait . . . or if—"

"It's all right, Shani." Mr. Foxe eagerly extracted the telegram and read out loud. "'April has been found here, in Traverse City. Letter with details follows. Love, M-R-V,' Minnie, Rosalie, and Vanda Mae," he explained before slapping Willy Jo on the back. "What do you know! April's been found way up in Michigan! At least now, we can put our minds to rest over that perplexity." When Willy Jo failed to smile, he asked, "What's the matter, son?"

"I can't help thinking . . ."

"Thinking what?"

"Eck Danvers is involved."

Mr. Foxe grew thoughtful. "Eck Danvers, your old nemesis? What makes you suspect him?"

"I'm sure he was lying to me the night April was stolen. I'm convinced he took her, and the other horses that have turned up missing hereabouts. I'd like to prove it."

Mr. Foxe pondered the suggestion. "I think you'd best tell your suspicions to my brother, since he's the sheriff. You're going to be too busy helping your daddy with the harvest to catch Danvers—if he *is* the thief."

As the buggy rolled into the carriage house, Willy Jo knew Mr. Foxe was right. Now was not the time to trail a horse thief. His daddy needed him, and no matter what his misgivings about moving home, he would not renege on the promise to return to the family farm.

CHAPTER 15

Vanda Mae rose at dawn, drew back the curtain, and sent up a silent prayer of thanks that this, the last Saturday in October, promised to be a day of sunshine. On her weekend visits home from the city, she needed every opportunity possible to prepare Topaz for the upcoming Fall Fair, and she couldn't afford a weekend of rain with the big horse show only six days off.

Sometimes, she still longed for April. The Morgan had been an exceptional horse, compliant and easy to work with. She wished April were here now, but she no longer begrudged Susan Reddick her ownership of the filly, nor her father's decision not to take the matter to court. Topaz had excellent qualities, and with her unusual markings, she just might find favor with the judges and win first place in the ladies' division.

After pulling on riding jacket, jodhpurs, and boots, Vanda Mae quietly slipped out of the manor house into the cool morning air and hurried toward the stable. Voices caught her attention before she even reached the open door—Gaspar's and another male voice she thought she recognized, though she hadn't heard it in more than two months. Then, the talking stopped, replaced by the sound of feet lightly landing on the wooden floor.

She stepped into the stable to discover the graceful acrobatics of the neighbor who'd disappeared back in August. Only now, Bobby Dan was performing more than simple handsprings down the center aisle, and he wasn't dressed in everyday shirt and pants. Clad in tights that revealed the muscular curves of his well-toned physique, he turned flips, back flips, twists, and handless cartwheels, threading himself through a huge ring held aloft by Gaspar, then coming to a halt two feet from her. As she and Gaspar applauded his tumbling run, Bobby Dan gave a bow, tossed back his fair hair, and offered her his winning smile.

"Bobby Dan! You're back!"

Quick as a wink he grabbed her by the shoulders, pecked her on the cheek, then set her free before she could register a protest. "Good to see you, Vanda Mae!" His blue eyes sparkled like never before, lighting up his entire countenance.

Slightly embarrassed by the sight of him in his skintight costume, she stumbled over her next words while keeping her gaze from wandering below his neck. "Are you . . . have you . . ."

Gaspar came up from behind, resting his hand in a fatherly fashion on Bobby Dan's shoulder. "Mr. Bobby and me, we make an act for the fair, *si?*"

Indicating a large wooden box at the opposite end of the aisle, Bobby Dan waxed enthusiastically. "Gaspar's reviving his famous escape act. I'm his assistant, then he's mine, when I do my acrobatics."

Grinning, Gaspar leveled his finger at her. "The Amazing Gaspar and Mr. Bobby every afternoon at Piedmont Park. Friday after horse show, you'll see!"

Vanda Mae clapped her hands. "I can hardly wait! Do your folks—"

Bobby Dan shook his head vigorously. "I haven't been home yet. I only got off the road last night. I came straight here to ask Gaspar if he'd team up with me."

"You've got to visit your folks. And Willy Jo. They'd love to see you!" she insisted.

The light in his eyes faded. "I can't. Not yet. If they want to see me, let them come to the fair and see my act."

One hand on her hip, finger wagging, Vanda Mae pinned him with a steadfast gaze. "Daddy won't stand for you hiding out here while your own mama and daddy are wanting to see you. I'm going right inside and tell him who I discovered in his stable."

No sooner had she pivoted on her heel than Bobby Dan caught her by the elbow and swung her back around. "All right, I'll go see them, but give me till tonight. Gaspar and I have a lot to do today, working up our act for the opening of the fair on Tuesday."

~~~

Willy Jo was helping his father fill the corn crib when a rider approached. The long shadows of the magnolias in late afternoon obscured the stranger from view at first. But when the fellow emerged in the sunlight at the end of the drive, Willy Jo knew the rider was no stranger after all.

"Daddy, look! It's Bobby Dan!"

Daddy's head snapped around. A grin burnished his tan features. Dropping his basket where he stood, he started toward his younger son with long, eager strides.

Willy Jo stayed put. As his brother drew closer, he could see that Bobby Dan appeared to be both fit and fine. The fact that he was on Topaz said that home hadn't been his first stop in the Piedmont. Willy Jo hurried to the house to fetch Mama from the kitchen where she and Kezia were preparing the evening meal. When he emerged with her a minute later, Bobby Dan had dismounted and was standing in the dooryard with Daddy's arm about his shoulders.

Mama smiled through her tears, evidently too overcome with happiness to do more than murmur his name before wrapping her arms about him. Releasing her embrace long moments later, she slipped one arm through his, the other through Willy Jo's. Her cheeks shimmering with moisture, she looked up into her younger son's face.

"This day is answered prayer. At last, my two boys are home with me again!"

Daddy's beaming smile lingered, too, and Willy Jo couldn't remember when he'd seen his folks this pleased. The years-long friction between him and his daddy had all but disappeared since his return from Tanglewood, and now the younger wayward son had come home. Even Willy Jo's own harsh feelings about Bobby Dan had dissipated with time, allowing him to forgive and forget past differences, and pray for his brother's wellbeing. Deep within, this reunion brought him peace—a peace instilled with the knowledge that God knows every need, and hears and answers prayers. The only flaw at this happy moment was the uncertainty in Bobby Dan's expression as his gaze met Willy Jo's.

He hastily offered words of reassurance. "Glad you're home, little brother. You'll stay to dinner—" Suddenly remembering his brother had just come off the road, and the sparse, primitive conditions of a traveling show, he amended his invitation. "You'll stay the night, won't you?"

"I'd like that," he quickly replied. Skepticism still evident on his brow, he quietly announced, "I've got news."

Suddenly dreading word of a betrothal to a trapeze artist, or some equally outlandish notion of his crazy little brother, Willy Jo forced himself to remain calm. "What's that, Bobby Dan?"

Lifting his nose to sniff the air, he winked mischievously. "I'll tell you over dinner. Right now, the smell of Kezia's sautéed onions and fried pork chops is making my mouth water. Do you know how long it's been since I've sat down to one of her home cooked meals?"

~~~

Thin clouds veiled the morning sun, dulling the reds and golds of the hardwoods trimming the road to Winston, but Willy Jo's vision remained clear regarding the race he intended to enter and win today at the fair.

In hand he held the reins to an exceptionally fine burnt chestnut stallion, Piedmont, a cross between a Morgan and an Arabian he had recently purchased with the money his father had paid him for his work on the farm. He wasn't quite the horse April had been, nor as expensive, but he was paid for in full, and he just might be fast enough to outrun the competition in the wagon race he'd decided to enter when his mother had refused to ride Piedmont in the ladies' competition.

With her decision firm and incontrovertible, Willy Jo had focused his efforts on the gentlemen's wagon race. The wagon in which he sat was very special without a doubt, an early birthday gift his folks had ordered built to specification at the Nissen Wagon Works. For a moment, his mind drifted, and instead of the cool, morning breeze teasing at his open collar, the rush of warm afternoon air whooshed by as he raced around the oval. Instead of the noisy, scolding grackles flocking to the maples as he drove along the country road, the crowd at Piedmont Park cheered him for coming in first at the finish line.

And he saw the fine, new buggy that would reward his success. His first buggy. His own buggy. A memento of practical worth that he could drive for years to come. How proud his daddy would be of him if he came away the owner of the best prize offered at the fair.

Smiling, he gazed heavenward and spoke reverently. "Lord, thank you for answering prayers, and teaching Daddy and me to get along. I didn't think you were listening, but now I know different." Seconds later, he added, "And Lord, if it wouldn't be too much to ask, help me get over the finish line before those other drivers."

Realizing how selfish his request sounded, he continued to pray in silence. *Lord, even if I don't win the wagon race, I know Daddy will still be proud of me. A few months back, I wouldn't have felt this way, but things are different now. Daddy's different. Sometimes, he even praises me. I know the words come hard for him. But thanks for putting them in his heart, and in his mouth.*

And like I said, I'd be mighty glad if I could win this race today, just so I could go up to him afterward and say, "Daddy, I did it for you!"

His focus shifted from private prayer to the handsome coach several yards in front of him carrying his daddy and mother. The carriage, with its double collar axles, patent leather dash, and Norway iron bolts, was drawn by the finest roans in all of Forsyth County. His daddy would enter the competition for the best pair of coach horses, outfit taken into account. The harness ornaments and plumes really made his rig stand out. Willy Jo was hoping his father would come away with the $15 prize being offered. If he did, he was certain his daddy would present his winnings to the woman on the seat beside him.

But winning was no sure thing with Mr. Foxe entering his own coach and horses in the Forsyth County event. Since horse thefts from Tanglewood had robbed him of his best team, Mr. Foxe had come up with a new pair. Willy Jo had seen them out on the road, and they were stylish indeed.

Willy Jo's musings of Tanglewood recalled his brother's appearance on Topaz and his surprise announcement. Thankfully, it had nothing to do with a young lady trapeze artist, or other betrothal. Instead, Bobby Dan had informed his family that he'd got up his own show in partnership with Gaspar, and they had contracted with the fair to give performances every afternoon at Piedmont Park. Then Bobby Dan had promptly insisted his folks wait until the end of the week when their act would be at its best before coming to see it.

So as Willy Jo neared the twin cities of Salem and Winston, this day was full of promise. The traffic heading into town on Main Street was far heavier than usual. Even Academy Square, several blocks from the hub of activity at the courthouse, seemed busier than normal.

He couldn't pass Salem Academy, its brick Main Hall or neighboring Home Church and steeple, without thinking of Vanda Mae. Bobby Dan had said she'd been home each weekend training to enter Topaz in the ladies' division of the horse show today, but Willy Jo hadn't seen or spoken with her since school had begun in September.

Willy Jo fondly recalled the rides he and Vanda Mae had taken together at Tanglewood. Her enthusiastic, eternally optimistic approach to life had set sunbeams dancing during days of discord with his father. But he hadn't forgotten the considerable frustration and worry inflicted by her daredevil nature. He supposed he never would understand why she would take chances on Steadmans' horse despite his—and her father's—warnings against it. But such was the way of Vanda Mae.

Despite her confounding spunkiness, thoughts of the young lady stirred an uneasiness deep within. Whether it was fondness, or guilt over his longtime friendship with her older sister, he couldn't tell. He'd been too busy with harvest on his daddy's farm to think much about Tanglewood women.

And thoughts of them now gave way to concerns for heavier traffic, both on foot and in wagons. The intersection at First Street, marked by the double porticos of the Sallade home, was bustling. Proceeding carefully, he negotiated the intersection at Second and approached the courthouse. Gaily decorated with a huge red and white bunting, it stood sentinel at Third and Main over an assortment of merchant booths that had been erected on the square. Even from the seat of his wagon, Mr. Seabott was touting the finer points of his Garland stoves to a woman with a white ruffled parasol and her silk-hatted husband. Beside them, the town optician, Mr. Harger, was examining the eyes of a frosty-haired prospect sporting bright red suspenders. Adjacent, Mr. Vogler promoted the finer points of his walnut sweetheart chest to a young couple more interested in gazing into each other's eyes, than into their reflections in his glossy varnish finish.

The fragrance of freshly pressed apple cider at Mr. Winkler's booth mingled with the less appetizing odor of horse and mule droppings in the congested street and the enticing aroma of freshly popped corn drifting from the popcorn wagon parked at the opposite curb.

No-name tunes from penny whistles, chimes of cowbells, and the occasional pop of a firecracker or discharge of a torpedo accented the symphony of happy voices, rattling wagons, and horses' hooves.

Slow going marked the block north of the courthouse where tobacco wagons lined both sides of the street in anticipation of offloading a new harvest at Brown's Warehouse. Willy Jo crept past Gentry's watchmaking shop, Farabee's restaurant and grocery, and Marler and Dalton's drygoods.

Once past the busiest section of Winston, Willy Jo followed his father's coach up Liberty Street, gaining a view of Pilot Mountain with its biscuit-like top. Thereafter, traffic moved at a better pace toward Piedmont Park. Though this end of town was busier than normal with dozens of extra hacks hired to shuttle folks from the city center to the outlying fairgrounds and back, Willy Jo was soon able to turn onto the county grounds.

While his daddy parked his coach near the show rings, Willy Jo turned in the direction of the race track. Entering through the passageway between the banks of bleachers, he saw the winner's prize on display at the center of the infield—a brand new buggy with solid silver trim, shiny brass lamps, and silky black fringe. A shiver rippled up Willy Jo's spine at the prospect of driving the classy carriage home.

As he approached the starting line, he counted six other wagons already lined up on the half-mile oval. He pulled even beside them. The driver to his left had his back to him as he performed a last-minute check of his tack. Willy Jo jumped down to do the same. He was inspecting Piedmont's belly band when the other fellow spoke, his voice both familiar and unwelcome.

"Young Winthrop, I expected you'd be driving a purebred Morgan, knowing your fondness for them."

In no hurry to respond, Willy Jo sensed Eck Danvers studying every detail of Piedmont and the new Nissen wagon. Deliberately, he turned to face him. Greeted by a sinister smile that said more than words, Willy Jo remained cool.

"Where you been, Danvers? Haven't seen you around these parts in awhile."

Danvers met his gaze briefly, then continued his assessment of Piedmont. "I've been away up North, but that ain't none—isn't any of your business."

Willy Jo suffered a near uncontrollable urge to grab the fellow's shirt with both fists and scream into his face, *You went to Chicago to auction off the horses you stole from Forsyth County, didn't you?* But calmer thinking brought an intriguing idea, and wiser course of action to mind.

Turning his attention to Danvers' outfit, he discovered a wagon that was small and light, and a bay Thoroughbred filly built powerful and lean enough to give it speed aplenty. Certain the horse couldn't have been off the track more than a few weeks, Willy Jo began to suffer misgivings over Piedmont's ability to match her. He spoke with complete confidence, nonetheless.

"I'll wave to you from the winner's circle when this is over, Danvers."

With a raised brow, Danvers replied, "I'll wave to *you* from the seat of that buggy when I drive it out of here, young Winthrop."

As the announcer warned contestants to prepare for the start of the race, Willy Jo said casually, "I understand the Foxe girl is entering her new Morgan in the ladies' competition. Blue ribbon horseflesh, from what I've seen."

With an air of studied disinterest, he replied, "I wish her well."

Aboard his wagon, Willy Jo tried not to hold Piedmont's reins too tight, but nerves tensed his grip. Before he could relax, the starting gun sounded.

CHAPTER 16

Danvers bolted down the track. The others followed close behind. But Willy Jo's horse remained frozen, blinded by a cloud of dust!

Willy Jo slapped the reins firmly against him. "Go, Piedmont, *go!*"

With a mighty lurch, he shot across the starting line and surged forth in a spirited gallop, pulling quickly into the middle of the pack.

But he was far back from the first turn when Danvers rounded it alone, his Thoroughbred pulling his wagon as if it were so much fluff.

Piedmont kept his stride, working his way to the front of the pack. By the second turn, he'd started to close in on Danvers.

Down the straightaway they flew, running neck and neck as Piedmont took the outside at the third turn.

Ahead briefly on the next straightaway, he attempted to pass the Thoroughbred.

She gave no quarter. Hugging the inside, she matched Piedmont's speed and bested it by a shoulder.

But Piedmont pressed hard. Going into the last turn, he ran even with the Thoroughbred, pulling ahead as they came out of it.

With the finish line in sight, Danvers continued his fight for the lead, pulling ahead by a nose. Then Willy Jo inched past him. Nose and nose, the lead alternated time and again. At the end, Willy Jo couldn't tell who had won.

Then he heard the voice of the announcer.

"And the winner is Willy Jo Winthrop!"

The crowd cheered. Willy Jo rounded the track in a victory lap. In the front row of the stands, his daddy waved his hat wildly, his face beaming with a pride of which Willy Jo had only dreamed.

Pulling onto the infield, he watched with satisfaction as the judge pinned a blue ribbon to Piedmont's bridle. Promising to collect his prize at the end of the day, he headed toward the exit where others were leaving to clear the way for the race to follow.

As he reached the passageway between the bleachers, Eck Danvers cut in front of him, pausing to doff his straw boater. "Hats off to you, young Winthrop. I didn't think that cross-breed horse of yours had it in him to win."

Willy Jo smiled. "You'd better find something faster than that Thoroughbred if you expect to take the prize next year."

With a covetous glance at Piedmont, Danvers asked, "You wouldn't be in the market to sell, would you?"

Willy Jo hooted in disbelief. "You never give up, do you?"

"Just thought I'd ask."

As Danvers drove out ahead of Willy Jo, more ideas emerged regarding his notion to catch a horse thief. But he couldn't dwell on them now. His daddy would soon be competing for the best pair of coach horses in ring eight, then Vanda Mae would be vying for Best Lady Rider in ring five.

He joined his mother and Mrs. Foxe to watch each coach and team take its turn as the center of attention. The first three carriages had been manufactured locally by Mr. Meinung, known for his drays and business wagons. These vehicles were practical and sturdy, but lacking the styling that could have made them stand out.

Next, his daddy entered the ring in his Cook carriage from New Haven, Connecticut. Its silk fringe tossed winsomely in the mild breeze, and his roans had never looked finer—their coats clean and shiny, their heads high and proud, their manes brushed to perfection. From the applause, he had easily won favor over the previous contestants.

Then Mr. Foxe made his grand entrance in a new Graham carriage from Rochester, New York. Its etched windows, sweeping fenders, and tall body made it a standout above all others, but Willy Jo was even more impressed by his neighbor's new team. They were the prettiest pair of matching dappled greys he'd ever seen, with their manes carefully braided, white plumes atop their heads, and silver studs on their harnesses and bridle fronts.

Onlookers clapped enthusiastically, and when the remaining contestants had been given their turn around the ring, the judge presented Mr. Foxe with the $15 prize.

He and Daddy joined Mrs. Foxe and Mama a few minutes later, Mr. Foxe offering Willy Jo a hearty pat on the back.

"Congratulations on your win, son!" To Daddy, he said, "Doesn't he make you proud?"

His daddy's face lit in a wide smile. "Proud as the day he was born." Playfully, he tapped Willy Jo's cheek with his fist, something his father had done hundreds of times to Bobby Dan, but never to him.

Suppressing an urge to hug his daddy right then and there, Willy Jo quickly changed topics. "We'd better get over to ring five if we want to see Vannie-Mae in the ladies' competition."

With new joy and a prayer of thankfulness in his heart, Willy Jo stood just outside the ring with his folks and the Foxes to watch each of the lady riders circle around at a walk, trot, and canter both in a clockwise and counterclockwise direction. The first four competitors were all much older than Vanda Mae. But each of their routines was flawed in some way. One had difficulty switching directions in the ring; another couldn't convince her horse to canter; the third horse balked, then nearly bolted into a canter; the fourth started to rear up, nearly dismounting its rider before going into its routine.

Throughout it all, each rider had a cluster of family and friends watching, and all of the onlookers outside the ring belonged to one of these groups—all except one. A fellow wearing a straw hat with a brim wide enough to shade his entire face changed his position each time a contestant finished her routine, lurking near the supporters of the new competitor, engaging them in casual conversation.

Now, Vanda Mae was standing just outside the ring. Her folks, and his alike, gave her their rapt attention, Mrs. Foxe waving and blowing a kiss to her daughter. Seconds later, the curious stranger stood but a few feet behind them.

Willy Jo turned to get a better look at the man, noting his full-bent pipe and the essence of his vanilla tobacco. Eager to engage the fellow in conversation, he edged nearer. "Have you got kin in this event?"

The stranger pushed back his hat, wiped his sweaty forehead with the cuff of his plaid shirt, and shook his head.
"Ain't from these parts." Indicating Vanda Mae, who was just
entering the ring, he asked, "Your sister?"

"Neighbor," Willy Jo replied, "from a farm called Tanglewood, on the line with Davidson County."

Though the fellow nodded casually, Willy Jo sensed he was
making note of the information even while easing away.

Having accomplished his objective, Willy Jo now turned
his complete attention to Vanda Mae. She was even more ap-
pealing than he remembered in her striking blue velvet jacket,
jodhpurs, and riding helmet, and with her hair in a braid that
bounced softly with each step of her mount. Topaz's mane and
tail had been braided also, with brightly colored satin ribbons.
Together, horse and rider created the prettiest picture Willy Jo
had ever seen.

And Vanda Mae's form was flawless. Her back was
straight and tilted forward at precisely the right angle; she
moved in perfect synchronization with Topaz, seeming one
with her horse; and the Morgan proceeded effortlessly and
flawlessly through each phase of her routine, following Vanda
Mae's quiet voice commands. When Topaz pranced out of the
ring, respectful applause registered the approval of her audience, including the curious stranger.

When two more contestants had performed in the ring, the
judge called Vanda Mae's name as the winner, presenting her
with the blue ribbon, a set of books containing classic litera-
ture, and the ten dollars that had been designated the prizes for
the ladies' competition. More applause followed. As she exited the ring, the stranger moved off.

Prizes in one hand, her horse's rein in the other, Vanda Mae joined her family and neighbors, her pretty oval face and shining blue eyes beaming. But she nearly ignored the compliments from her folks to focus with excitement on Willy Jo.

"You did it! You won the buggy! I'm so happy for you!" Impetuously, she dropped Topaz's rein, shoved her books and money into her father's hands, and put her arms lightly about Willy Jo's neck to peck his cheek.

Willy Jo was too stunned for words, his face burning in response.

Mr. Foxe chuckled. "That's one prize you hadn't counted on, eh, son?"

Vanda Mae waved her hand. "Don't pay Daddy any mind, Willy Jo."

Jabe said, "Seems to me, for a kiss like that, the least a fella can do is give the young lady a ride in his new buggy."

Vanda Mae's brow rose. "Would you, Willy Jo? This weekend, before I go back to Aunt Ophelia and Uncle George's for school?"

Willy Jo nodded.

Mrs. Foxe said, "Maybe he'll carry you back to your aunt and uncle's, come Sunday afternoon."

Willy Jo's mama said, "I'm sure he would. Wouldn't you, dear?" She touched her gloved hand to his wrist.

Still recovering from his embarrassment, he replied, "I'd be honored to carry you, Vannie-Mae. What time should I fetch you?"

She shrugged. "Two o'clock?"

As quickly as her enthusiasm had swelled for the buggy ride, it seemed to die, her attention now distracted by activity in the ring to their left. "Look! It's Bobby Dan and Gaspar!

They're about to start their act!" Taking Topaz's rein in hand once more, she headed in that direction.

Willy Jo and the others followed, forming the nucleus of an audience that grew as Bobby Dan, clad in leotard and tights, performed a series of handsprings the circumference of the ring to music performed by an accordionist. As the tempo increased, so did the speed of his handsprings, until he made his way to a trunk set in the center of the ring, performing a back flip, then a front flip over the wooden chest.

With a chord sounding like "ta-da" from the accordionist, the audience applauded, then Bobby Dan made an announcement.

"Good afternoon, ladies, and gentlemen! I'm Bobby Dan, and I'd like to introduce to you my partner, the amazing Gaspar, escape artist extraordinaire!"

Dressed in black pants, a red silk shirt, and a sash reminiscent of the garb worn by bullfighters, Gaspar hurried to the center of the ring, bowing deeply to another smattering of applause while flourishes sounded from the accordion.

Gaspar opened the trunk and removed a rope, a canvas bag, a chain, a padlock, and a silk sheet. To the suspenseful notes of the musician, Bobby Dan tied Gaspar's hands behind his back, chained and locked the canvas bag, and closed him inside the trunk. He then wrapped a chain around the trunk and secured it with a padlock, finally draping it with the silk sheet. While the accordionist began to slowly play *Pop! Goes the Weasel,* Bobby Dan started performing cartwheels around the circle, slowly at first, then faster as the music gained tempo.

Willy Jo found the acrobatics simple and unimaginative—far below his brother's capabilities. But as the tempo of the music picked up, so did the speed of his brother's gymnastics until Bobby Dan was speeding toward the center of the ring in a series of handless cartwheels. Hurling himself in a high forward flip over the trunk, he'd barely cleared it when Gaspar burst forth from beneath the silk sheet to the *Pop!* at the end of the song.

The audience applauded enthusiastically, especially the children. Then the accordion player struck up a new melody while Bobby Dan and Gaspar carried a lightweight folding screen to the center of the ring. Starting behind the trunk, they set it in place around three sides, leaving the chest visible only from the front. To the notes of a haunting melody, Bobby Dan again tied Gaspar's hands behind his back, chained and locked him inside the canvas bag, then closed him inside the trunk, chaining it and locking it no less than four times.

Now, to low and mysterious tones from the accordion, Bobby Dan drew the silk screen closed and stepped behind it. After a moment's pause, the accordionist played a chord filled with expectation. When nothing happened, he progressed to a chord one step higher. More silence. Then he sounded a third, triumphant chord, fortissimo, but still, no one appeared from behind the screen.

Perspiration trickled from Willy Jo's forehead. Obviously something had gone terribly wrong. The musician, appearing much distressed, sounded his chord again.

Just when murmurs of skepticism began rippling through the audience, Gaspar pulled back the screen and revealed himself to the crowd with great finesse, the accordionist enhancing the moment with his most triumphant chord yet.

But only moments later, some in the audience began calling out to Gaspar.

"Where's Bobby Dan?"

"Where's your partner?"

With great pretense to sudden memory, Gaspar hurried to the trunk. Using the flair of a seasoned showman, he unlocked the four chains, raising his hands in the air after each one, then again when he opened the lid of the trunk. Inside, a figure in the canvas bag tried to poke his way out. Gaspar helped the shrouded fellow to his feet and unlocked the chain at the top of the bag.

Out stepped Bobby Dan, his hands tied behind his back.

Applause, loud and furious, filled the air. The accordionist lit into a series of ruffles and flourishes. Gaspar untied Bobby Dan's hands. Performing one last cartwheel and flip, he and his partner bowed, then made a swift exit, props in tow.

Jabe hollered, "Good show, Bobby Dan!"

Willy Jo had never seen such delight in his mother's eyes, nor heard such loud applause from a pair of gloved hands.

Vanda Mae's folks were nearly as enthusiastic as his own. Mr. Foxe said, "I hope Gaspar doesn't take a notion to go back on the road. I could never replace him at the stables."

Vanda Mae was the last to stop clapping. Her face aglow, she told Willy Jo, "I'm so proud of Bobby Dan! Aren't you?"

He nodded. Certainly the grin on his face was enough to convey the sentiment in his heart. For years, he'd considered Bobby Dan's shenanigans and acrobatics a pure waste, just a way to avoid his share of chores around the farm. He couldn't be more pleased to know that the tumbling tricks and practical jokes had paid off.

Mr. Foxe checked his watch, then drew his wife and Vanda Mae to him. "It's getting late, ladies. What do you say we call it a day at the fair?" Seeing their nods of agreement, he turned to the Winthrops, his gaze taking in the three of them. "How about following us to Tanglewood for dinner? I'll stop by the lumber yard office so Minnie can ring up Shani and tell her to toss three more yams into the pot."

Willy Jo waited hopefully for his father's response.

Daddy's focus took in Mama and Willy Jo. "That'd be a right hospitable end to our day, don't ya think?" Receiving their approval, he told Mr. Foxe, "Why don't ya head over to the lumber yard to ring home. Meanwhile, I'll help Willy Jo hitch his new buggy to the back of his wagon, then we'll be right along."

As Willy Jo followed the Foxes and his daddy out of town, he recalled his trip down the same road several weeks earlier, on the first weekend in August, when he was returning with his mother, brother, and Vanda Mae from the trolley party. Crossing paths with Danvers today, then seeing the stranger lurking near the lady competitors conjured up bad memories— thoughts of Vanda Mae's first Morgan being stolen in Salem; the pure terror that had ripped through his heart when a crazy horseback rider had come up behind him shooting off a gun; the immediate arrival of Danvers on the scene; and his suspicious-sounding denials when asked about the rider and Topaz.

Of course, there was no danger of Topaz being stolen tonight. She was safely hitched to the back of Mr. Foxe's coach. And as for being run off the road, dusk was only starting to fall. A gun-toting horseman wouldn't strike without full cover of darkness. Besides, Willy Jo's wagon wasn't a lone vehicle on a deserted road as had been the situation in August.

More than ever, he was certain Danvers, the lone horseman of that fateful August night, and the stranger lurking about at the horse show were somehow connected, and responsible for the thefts of many Forsyth County horses in earlier months.

The problem was catching them in the act. And Willy Jo had been laying bait for that very possibility all day.

After dinner, when his daddy and Mr. Foxe withdrew to the library, he'd talk to them. Despite the fact that Danvers had caused a great rift between him and his daddy in the past, he believed their respect for one another had grown deep enough that now, Daddy would listen to what he had to say about the man.

~~~

Sipping hot mulled cider after a filling meal, Willy Jo set his cup on the library table and waited for the banter about the prices of hogs and lumber between his father and Mr. Foxe to break off. Drawing a breath of air heavy with smoke from their cigars, Willy Jo squared his shoulders and took advantage of the rare moment of silence following the men's laughter.

"Daddy, Mr. Foxe, there's something I'd like to discuss with you."

Mr. Foxe flicked the ashes from his cigar into the tray beside his winged leather chair and leaned forward, his smile fading. "Sounds serious."

Daddy exhaled smoke in tiny rings that drifted toward the plaster medallion above the fan and chandelier, then focused on Willy Jo. "Go ahead, son."

"Today, I noticed a real suspicious-looking fellow at the ladies' competition." He explained the hints he'd dropped to the fellow about Tanglewood, and to Danvers about Vanda Mae's new Morgan, because of his long-held conviction that the man was behind the previous thefts. Then he told of his concern that the fellows could be in cahoots to steal Topaz this very night.

His father's brow creased. "We've got no real evidence that Danvers steals horses. And as for that other fellow, he's probably just a stranger in town for the fair like hundreds of others."

Mr. Foxe's gaze met Willy Jo's. "Even if he *is* planning to get his hands on someone else's horse, how do we know he'll come *here* tonight? He could have his sights set on any one of those other ladies' mounts."

Willy Jo pressed ahead. "You could be right, but I think he'll go for the best horse first. What I'd like to do is turn Topaz out to pasture for tonight and set up a blind there, a haystack beside the far gate. That way, I can keep my eye on the horse, and on anybody coming to steal her."

Mr. Foxe and Daddy exchanged glances, their skepticism obvious. Then, with a chuckle, Mr. Foxe said, "You're young. If you want to give up a good night's sleep, I won't object, but I think it's all for naught."

CHAPTER 17

Two hours later, while Mama and Daddy were engrossed in their game of charades with the Foxes in the manor house parlor, Willy Jo took up his lone watch in Topaz's pasture from within the confines of a mound of hay. He'd been settled inside his haystack by the gate farthest from the stables for less than an hour when he began to question the wisdom of his plan. He could see very little in the dark of night, clouds obscuring moon and stars, and the bare skin on his hands and neck had begun to itch. He'd suffered a sneezing fit that had turned his handkerchief into a wet rag, and despite the layer of clothing protecting the rest of his body, he imagined pin-head-sized bugs crawling all over him, making him itch like mad and eager to head for the nearest tub of bath water.

He'd played in haystacks plenty of times as a small boy and never itched so badly. And as an adult, he hadn't been particularly bothered by hay when feeding horses, with the exception of an occasional sneeze which he'd blamed on dust. But this close, prolonged contact was definitely bringing out the worst in him.

To pass the time and put discomfort from mind, he began silently recalling Bible verses he'd memorized as a child. Several had come to mind when he paused to ponder one of his favorites.

For God so loved the world, that he gave his only begotten Son, that whosoever believeth in him should not perish, but have everlasting life. John 3:16.

He considered this to be the greatest message in all the Bible—that long ago, God had become the father of Jesus, nurturing and loving him from infancy to manhood; that God had endowed his son with an important mission—to bring His love to all the world; that God had sacrificed his precious son in a cruel, painful death on the cross.

Willy Jo closed his eyes and thanked God for his own redemption through Christ, the enduring friendship Jesus offered to all, and the workings of the Savior's love in his own heart, and his daddy's. Truly, through Christ all things were possible, even the reconciliation with his daddy that had seemed inconceivable. Dark days and nights of conflict had given way to brighter, happier times for them both.

His thoughts were interrupted by the faint rumbling of thunder in the distance. Topaz was growing uneasy, pacing back and forth inside the closed gate that kept her from entering the stable. Sprinkles of rain began to fall, then larger drops. The wind gusted stronger, tugging at the hay mound.

Lightning flashed, thunder cracked loud overhead, and rain fell hard. A mighty gust of wind stole the last of Willy Jo's hay mound leaving him totally exposed. Head down, he ran across the pasture and whipped open the gate for a frantic Topaz, following her into the stable where he put her in her box and wiped her down. Damp and discouraged, but not defeated, he was determined to return to the pasture when the storm had passed.

He checked the time—nearly one in the morning. The lights in the windows of the manor house told him the parlor games continued on. The same was true an hour later when he turned Topaz out to pasture again and reconstructed his hay mound, this time under clear skies in a field lit by both moon and stars.

The temperature dropped as the hours passed. The storm had brought cooler air, and despite the thick layer of hay blanketing him on all sides, Willy Jo grew chilled in his damp clothing.

With an hour left till dawn, his throat grew sore. Surely a head cold would follow. His eyes burred from exhaustion, his neck and back tightened with knots, and his patience had nearly run out.

Daddy and Mr. Foxe had been right. He'd wasted a good night's sleep. He rubbed his eyes. Visions of the warm, dry bed waiting for him at home came to mind. Ready to admit defeat and give up his foolish vigil, he made one last perusal of the pasture.

A man was sneaking past the far gate.

Willy Jo's heart skipped a beat. Wide awake and keenly alert, he watched the fellow carrying something toward Topaz where she stood sleeping at the opposite side of the pasture. In the blink of an eye, he'd slipped a halter over the Morgan's head, a bag over that, and began leading her away.

When he passed close to the haystack, Willy Jo caught a whiff of his vanilla pipe tobacco, and detected the silhouette of his wide-brimmed straw hat. Surely this man was the same fellow he'd seen lurking about the ladies' competition. After he and Topaz had left the pasture, Willy Jo shadowed them, hiding in the fringe of trees along the road. He'd followed for a quarter of a mile when the thief headed off the road into the woods.

Willy Jo hurried to catch up. There, in a small clearing lit by dim lantern light, stood a large livestock van. Three horses were already aboard, and beside the rear entry ramp waited another man.

Eck Danvers.

He opened the gate to the van while his accomplice started leading Topaz up its ramp.

Willy Jo charged into the open.

"Stop! You can't get away with this!"

In a flash, Danvers pulled a pistol from beneath his jacket and turned it on Willy Jo. "Hold it right there, young Winthrop!"

Willy Jo froze.

To his assistant, Danvers said, "Fitch, get the Morgan aboard. We've got to do something about young Winthrop, here." He smiled wickedly.

Willy Jo started to back away.

"Stay put!" Danvers ordered, cocking the hammer of his gun. "Do as I say, and you won't get hurt. Run, and you're a dead man."

Willy Jo's mind raced, desperate for a means of escape. If only he could run back to the house and call for help! But with Danvers' focus steady upon him, he couldn't move.

Then, he heard horses coming down the road. Danvers heard them too. The instant his gaze turned toward the sound, Willy Jo rushed at him, tackling him by the legs.

Danvers hit the ground with a thud.

A shot went off.

A horse wailed. Had Topaz been shot? Willy Jo looked up.

Danvers took advantage. Still holding the gun, he rolled on top of Willy Jo and forced the pistol against his neck. "I'm losing patience with you, young Winthrop! Your next move is your last!" To Fitch, he said, "Get me the rope in the van!"

A few feet away, a horse continued to whinny and Fitch struggled with Topaz.

"Get the blame rope yourself!" Fitch retorted.

"I said get the rope!" Danvers hollered. *"Now!"*

Before Fitch could reply, Daddy and Mr. Foxe burst into the clearing aboard Hurricane and Firelight.

Danvers turned his gun on them.

With a mighty effort, Willy Jo pushed him off, knocked his pistol away, and straddled him, pinning his shoulders to the ground.

Daddy dismounted in an instant, lending his strength to hold Danvers still.

Fitch scrambled to shut the van gate.

Mr. Foxe retrieved the pistol and pointed it at him. "Get away from there, you thief!"

Fitch put his hands up. "I only did what Danvers told me! It was all his idea!" He took a step back.

"Stop right there!" Mr. Foxe warned.

Daddy brought Danvers to his feet and slammed him up against the side of the van. "You rotten, good-for-nothin' . . ." To Willy Jo, he said, "I should've listened to ya from the start, son. Ya were right all along about this no-account."

Fitch spoke again. "He's been stealin' from places all 'round this county for months."

Danvers strained against Daddy's hold. "Shut your mouth, Fitch!"

Daddy tightened his grip. *"You* hush!"

To Willy Jo, Fitch said, "Danvers made me spy on you and the young lady in the woods last summer."

Willy Jo, recalled his sense of being trailed during his rides with Vanda Mae.

Fitch continued. "And the night he made me steal that Morgan from Salem, he saw a chance to heist your daddy's drivin' team and told me to run ya off the road."

"It's a lie!" Danvers claimed.

"No, it ain't! You figerred to make a big accident. Told me to unhitch the horses while the folks was too hurt to stop me."

Daddy went for Danvers' throat. "You . . ."

He struggled for air, his eyes bulging.

Willy Jo moved to ease his daddy's grip. "No good will come of strangling him."

Daddy loosened his hold.

Fitch went on. "When the buggy didn't turn over, he rode by and offered to help ya just to make ya think he was a good S'maritan."

Willy Jo pinned his gaze on Danvers. "You took the Morgan to Chicago and sold her at auction, didn't you?"

Fitch answered for him. "He did! And a carload of other horses, too. Put hisself in tall cotton!"

Daddy put his face inches from Danvers. "There's one thing I don't understand. In the beginnin', ya were willin' to buy that Morgan and pay a mighty big price for her."

Danvers' mouth twitched but he made no reply.

His accomplice explained. "He'd a paid somethin' down and given ya a promissory note for the rest."

"I'd have never taken a note," Daddy declared.

Fitch chortled. "Ya woulda from *him*. He can talk the bone away from a dog! And that woulda been the last y'd a seen of him, *and* your horse."

"If Danvers wanted the Morgan so much, why did he auction her off?" Willy Jo asked.

Again, Fitch's derisive laugh cut the air. "He changes his mind 'bout horses quicker 'n flames scorch feathers."

With a wave of the pistol, Mr. Foxe motioned Fitch toward his boss. "Get over there so we can tie the two of you together. One thing's not going to change. You're both on your way to the pokey and my brother—the sheriff—will be mighty glad to see you."

Willy Jo quickly found the rope in the van, discovering with relief that Topaz had not been shot. Rather, the horse in front of her had been grazed in the rear.

As he helped his father tie the culprits together, a puzzling question came to mind regarding Mr. Foxe and his daddy.

"How is it you happened to show up just when I needed you?"

Daddy offered a wry smile. "A couple of hours ago, three worried women shamed us into watchin' the meadow from the stable."

In his heart, Willy Jo interpreted the answer to mean *three worried women with the voice of God.*

CHAPTER 18

Willy Jo's gut tightened as Rosalie Foxe opened the door to welcome his family to their traditional day-after-Thanksgiving potluck buffet. After a holiday filled with Winthrop family aunts, uncles, and cousins, and a feast that produced leftovers too abundant and delicious to be fed to the hogs, the neighborly get-together had become a yearly, less formal luncheon he had cherished from childhood.

But this year, it held special meaning. It would be the first time he'd seen Rosalie since she'd left for Michigan at the start of the summer. His gaze met hers, and she offered a tentative smile. He returned an equally uncertain one. The awkward moment passed when Mama entered the foyer.

She took Rosalie's hand in hers. "Welcome home, honey! It's so good to see you. You look wonderful!" She brushed a kiss against Rosalie's cheek.

Rosalie returned the affection. "And you, Mrs. Winth- rop."

Bobby Dan followed Mama inside. His impish grin firmly in place, he reached into his jacket. "I've brought you a little present!" Out popped a huge bouquet of silk flowers.

Rosalie laughed. "I can see you're as tricky as you ever were, Bobby Dan."

Daddy entered on Bobby Dan's heels. "Trickier, if that's possible. Hello, Rosalie. You're lookin'well."

"Likewise, Mr. Winthrop."

He passed through the foyer leaving Willy Jo and Rosalie alone. Willy Jo gazed into her eyes, her familiar brown ones reflecting his own nervous anticipation. Undercurrents of conversation drifted from the parlor as Vanda Mae and her folks welcomed Willy Jo's family, but for the moment, Willy Jo stood tongue-tied.

On past holidays, long separations at school had prompted prolific conversation. But not today. They were students no longer, and the distance between them was beginning to resemble the Yadkin, wide and silent.

But even the Yadkin was bridgeable, and when Willy Jo finally found the right words, they erupted in spurts, nearly colliding with Rosalie's.

"You're looking well," she said.

"You're looking fine."

"It's nice to be home." She nibbled her lower lip.

"Good to have you back." He shifted his weight, sensing her regard for him had shifted as well.

She gestured toward the parlor. "Let's join the others. The buffet will be ready soon."

In the parlor, though Rosalie took the chair beside his, her focus turned to the Bobby Dan and the card trick he was performing. When he finished, applause filled the room.

Later, at the dining table, Willy Jo was restrained as Vanda Mae drew stories from Bobby Dan about his experiences as an itinerant performer. But when Daddy took up the subject of hog farming, Willy Jo shared his opinion willingly and confidently. And Daddy listened intently.

As the meal neared an end, the topic turned to horses. Mrs. Foxe set down her fork and laid aside her napkin, making an observation. "I know of at least four horses in the meadow that would love some exercise on the trail through the woods, and I think you young folks ought to take it upon yourselves to grant their wish."

Vanda Mae was the first to respond. "I can't think of a better way to spend the afternoon! If I may be excused—"

Mrs. Foxe waved her off. "Go! All of you! And leave us older folks to our parlor games."

Willy Jo helped Gaspar and Bobby Dan bring the horses into the stable and saddle them while Rosalie and Vanda Mae changed into suitable riding attire. So many years had passed since he'd seen Rosalie on horseback that he was unable to imagine it now, but he prepared Mr. Foxe's most docile standard-bred mare—a pretty, wide-backed sorrel—with care to ensure that the bit and bridle were properly adjusted and the sidesaddle wouldn't slip. He was tightening the saddle on Hurricane, and Bobby Dan was doing the same for Topaz when Rosalie and Vanda Mae joined them.

"Let's ride down by the river," said Rosalie. "It's been nearly half a year since I've seen it."

Bobby Dan chuckled. "Same for me. We ought to check and see if it's still there."

Vanda Mae laughed. "If not, you ought to add that to your repertoire of magic tricks—making a river change its course!"

He pulled a wry smile. "Come on, Miss Champion of Forsyth County, I'll give you a hand up."

They were on their horses and gone in an instant, leaving Willy Jo eager to dash after them. He ignored the urge, patiently helping Rosalie mount the sorrel, which she accomplished with much greater ease, grace, and expediency than he had anticipated, considering her cumbersome riding habit and crippled right arm.

He found nothing cumbersome in her riding style, however. Trotting beside him, she crossed the meadow with a confidence and form that betrayed no evidence of her long held fear of horses. When they came to the gate at the opposite side, he dismounted to open it for her.

She quickly passed through, telling him, "You take the lead, Willy Jo. You know the river paths far better than I."

As he walked Tassie into the woods, he couldn't help recalling the times he'd been there with Vanda Mae, nor wishing she were the one riding behind him now. Glancing back at Rosalie, he suffered a sharp pang of guilt. After all their years of cherished friendship, after all the time she'd just spent up North, he should be thrilled to have her near. Instead, he could hardly think of a thing to say. And although she was making small talk about her aunt and uncle in Michigan, he could barely concentrate on her words, instead hearing Bobby Dan and Vanda Mae ahead of them on the path, their laughter drifting to him on the cool, gusty breeze that stirred new fallen leaves beneath naked trees.

Rosalie called to him. "Willy Jo, I'd like to stop for awhile by the river."

Though he longed to continue down the path toward Bobby Dan and her sister, he nodded, and without a word, dismounted and helped her down.

They watched the water laze its way downstream, tasted the sweet tanginess of a muscadine that had dried on its vine, and listened to the echoing voices of Vanda Mae and Bobby Dan as they shouted nonsense across the water.

"Things surely are different than I remember," said Rosalie

Looking past her to the watery scene, he shrugged. "The river seems the same to me, except maybe the reflection of the trees now that fall's come."

"I wasn't referring to the river, Willy Jo," she said quietly. "I was referring to us. We were the same for so many years, the best of friends." Looking deep into his eyes, she added, "Though neither of us ever admitted it, we had assumptions about the future—that we'd always be together."

He couldn't mistake the sadness in her words. Struggling for a reply, he drew a tight breath.

She smiled and continued. "Like I said, things are different now." Her tone suddenly light, she talked on. "We've gone in separate directions. Other people and places have become important, where they weren't before."

Willy Jo reached for her hand. Though he'd known for months that Rosalie had struck up a friendship with a lawyer in Michigan, and he was pleased for her, he couldn't squelch the recurring guilt that her very own sister was stealing his heart.

Her gaze searched his with a depth he'd not seen before. "In the time we've been apart, I can see you've grown fond of Vanda Mae. I can't think of anyone I'd rather have sweet on my sister than you, Willy Jo."

His brow lifted. "You knew?"

She gave his hand an affectionate squeeze. "It's more obvious than you think."

Breaking off contact, he propped his foot on a stump and leaned his elbow on his knee. Chin in hand, he regarded her thoughtfully. "You're sweet on a gentleman up North." Seeing her momentary discomfort, he said quickly, "Michigan agrees with you. When are you going back?" Suddenly flustered over his inept question, he stammered. "I . . . I didn't mean that the way it sounded."

She chuckled. "Sending me packing already, are you?"

Warmth flooded his face. He hung his head. The touch of her cool, gloved finger beneath his chin stemmed his embarrassment. When he met her gaze now, he found joy and anticipation glimmering in her eyes.

"I'm leaving the day after tomorrow. I'll be spending Christmas there. Aunt Lottie and Uncle Ben need my help in their candy shop."

"And a certain lawyer friend will be more than pleased that you will be spending the holiday with him, I presume."

She grinned. "I presume."

Vanda Mae and Bobby Dan approached on the trail, and she spoke again. "It's time you and I swap riding partners. You ride back with Vanda Mae. I'll go with your brother."

CHAPTER 19

Following the Christmas Eve service in Salem, Willy Jo escorted Vanda Mae out into the still night. His hand at her elbow, he paused to peer into her eyes. "May I speak with you alone, Vannie-Mae?"

With a word to her relatives that she would join them in a minute, she allowed him to escort her to a more private place in front of the ivy-clad Main Hall of Salem Academy. Across the street, moonlight poured down on Academy Square tracing bare elms and sycamores in black against the starry sky and glistening off the white dormers of the neighboring Inspector's House.

Willy Jo reached inside his coat and produced a small rectangular box which he pressed into Vannie-Mae's hand. "I wanted you to have this before tomorrow."

In the gaslight, she stared down at the gold embossing against the black cover and read the words out loud. "Wm. T. Vogler, Jeweler. You shouldn't have done this, Willy Jo. I have nothing for you."

"Open it, Vannie-Mae," he quietly urged.

"But—"

"Open it."

She impatiently worked the tight-fitting cover free. There, nestled in cotton, lay a miniature silver horse with shimmering gemstone eyes. With a tiny gasp, she carefully lifted it from its bed.

"The eyes are topaz chips," he informed her.

She smiled up at him. "Willy Jo, I hardly know what to say."

He shifted his weight. "Next summer, when the Academy lets out, maybe we can take some rides by the river again."

"I'll look forward to it. Thank you, for the invitation *and* the gift. Merry Christmas, Willy Jo!"

He grinned. "Merry Christmas, Vannie-Mae!"

As he ushered her back to the company of her relatives, then slipped away in the silent darkness, he thanked God for the promise of good times to come.

CHAPTER 20

June 1901

Willy Jo watched Vannie-Mae intently from his usher's post at the rear of the small congregation in the Foxe's rose garden, where their relatives and friends had gathered for Rosalie's wedding. Though Rosalie and the lawyer from Traverse City were exchanging vows this day, he envisioned a time about two years off when he and Vannie-Mae would be the ones pledging promises of a lifetime. She'd be finished at the Academy then. It would give him just enough time to get established as a full partner in his daddy's hog farming business and put up a pretty house for his bride. His daddy had already given him the plat next to his folks' place to build on, and Mr. Foxe had offered to provide lumber and labor at cost as soon as he was ready to break ground. Reflecting on the days when Vannie-Mae and Bobby Dan had been best of friends and both families had assumed he himself would one day marry Rosalie, Willy Jo marveled at God's infinite wisdom and power in guiding and blessing those who truly seek and love Him.

ABOUT DONNA WINTERS

Donna adopted Michigan as her home state in 1971 when she moved there from a small town outside of Rochester, New York. She began penning novels in 1982 while working full time for an electronics company in Grand Rapids.

She resigned in 1984 following a contract offer for her first book. Since then, she has written several romance novels for various publishers, including Thomas Nelson Publishers, Zondervan Publishing House, Guideposts, and Bigwater Publishing LLC. Her nonfiction writing has been published by Chalfont House.

Her husband, Fred, an American History teacher, shares her enthusiasm for history. Together, they visit historical sites, restored villages, museums, and lake ports, purchasing books and reference materials and taking photos. She has visited Traverse City and walked the historic streets on many occasions since her first acquaintance with the city in 1968. . A trip to the Con Foster Museum in Traverse City provided valuable insights regarding turn-of-the-century Grand Traverse Bay and its resorts.

Donna has lived all of her life in states bordering on the Great Lakes. Her familiarity and fascination with these remarkable inland waters and her residence in the heart of Great Lakes Country provide the perfect background for writing *Great Lakes Romances*®.

MORE GREAT LAKES ROMANCES®

Visit
www.GreatLakesRomances.com
for excerpts and pricing.

Mackinac, *First in the series of Great Lakes Romances®* (Set at Grand Hotel, Mackinac Island, 1895.) Victoria Whitmore is no shy, retiring miss. When her father runs into money trouble, she heads to Mackinac Island to collect payment due from Grand Hotel for the furniture he's made. But dealing with Rand Bartlett, the hotel's manager, poses an unexpected challenge. Can Victoria succeed in finances without losing her heart?

The Captain and the Widow, Second in the series of Great Lakes Romances® (Set in South Haven, Michigan, 1897.) Lily Atwood Haynes is beautiful, intelligent, and alone at the helm of a shipping company at the tender age of twenty. Then Captain Hoyt Curtiss offers to help her navigate the choppy waters of widowhood. Together, can they keep a new shipping line—and romance—afloat?

Sweethearts of Sleeping Bear Bay, Third in the series of Great Lakes Romances® (Set in the Sleeping Bear Dune region of northern Michigan, 1898.) Mary Ellen Jenkins has successfully mastered the ever-changing shoals and swift currents of the Mississippi, but Lake Michigan poses a new set of challenges. Can she round the ever-dangerous Sleeping Bear Point in safety, or will the steamer—and her heart—run aground under the influence of Thad Grant?

Charlotte of South Manitou Island, Fourth in the series of Great Lakes Romances ® (Set on South Manitou Island, Michigan, 1891-1898) Charlotte Richards, fatherless at age eleven, thought she'd never smile again. But Seth Trevelyn, son of South Manitou Island's lightkeeper, makes it his mission to show her that life goes on, and so does true friendship. Together, they explore the World's Columbian Exposition in far-away Chicago where he saves her from a near-fatal fire. When he leaves the island to create a life of his own in Detroit, he realizes Charlotte is his one true love. Will his feelings be returned when she grows to womanhood?

Aurora of North Manitou Island, Fifth in the series of Great Lakes Romances® (Set on North Manitou Island, Michigan, 1898-1899.) With her new husband, Harrison, lying helpless after an accident on stormy Lake Michigan, Aurora finds marriage far from the glorious romantic adventure she had anticipated. And when Serilda Anders appears out of his past to tend the light and nurse him to health, Aurora is certain her marriage is doomed. Maybe Cad Blackburn, with the ready wit and silver tongue, is the answer. But it isn't right to accept the safe harbor he's offering. Where is the light that will guide her through troubled waters?

Bridget of Cat's Head Point, Sixth in the series of Great Lakes Romances® (Set in Traverse City and the Leelanau Peninsula of Michigan, 1899-1900.) When Bridget Richards leaves South Manitou Island to take up residence on Michigan's mainland, she suffers no lack of ardent suitors. Nat Trevelyn wants desperately to make her his bride and the mother of his two-year-old son. Attorney Kenton McCune showers her with gifts and rapt attention. And Erik Olson shows her the incomparable beauty and romance of a Leelanau summer. Who will finally win her heart?

Queen City Candy Shoppe (excerpted from Rosalie of Grand Traverse Bay), Seventh in the series of Great Lakes Romances® (Set in Traverse City, Michigan, 1900.) Soon after Rosalie Foxe arrives in Traverse City for the summer of 1900, she stands at the center of controversy. Her aunt and uncle are about to lose their confectionery shop, and Rosalie is being blamed. Can Kenton McCune, a handsome, Harvard-trained lawyer, prove her innocence and win her heart?

Isabelle's Inning, Encore Edition #1 in the series of Great Lakes Romances® (Set in the heart of Great Lakes Country, 1903.) Born and raised in the heart of the Great Lakes, Isabelle Dorlon pays little attention to the baseball players patronizing her mother's rooming house—until Jack Weatherby moves in. He's determined to earn a position with the Erskine College Purple Stockings, and a place in her heart as well, but will his affections fade once he learns the truth about her humiliating flaw?

Jenny of L'Anse Bay, Special Edition in the series of Great Lakes Romances® (Set in the Keweenaw Peninsula of Upper Michigan in 1867.) Eager to escape the fiery disaster that leaves her home in ashes, Jennifer Crawford sets out on an adventure to an Ojibway Mission on L'Anse Bay. In the wilderness, her affections grow for a native people very different from herself—especially for the chief's son, Hawk. Together, can they overcome the differences of their diverse cultures, and the harsh, deadly weather of the North Country?

Elizabeth of Saginaw Bay, Pioneer Edition in the series of Great Lakes Romances® (Set in the Saginaw Valley of Michigan, 1837.) The taste of wedding cake is still sweet in Elizabeth Morgan's mouth when she sets out with her bridegroom, Jacob, from York State for the new State of Michigan. But she isn't prepared for the untamed forest, crude lodgings, and dangerous diseases that await her there. Desperately, she seeks her way out of the forest that holds her captive, but God seems to have another plan for her future.

Unlikely Duet—Caledonia Chronicles—Part 1 in the series of Great Lakes Romances® (Set in Caledonia, Michigan, 1905.) Caroline Chappell practiced long and hard for her recital on the piano and organ in Caledonia's Methodist Episcopal Church. She even took up the trumpet and composed a duet to perform with Joshua Bolden, an ace trumpet player whom she'd long admired. Now, two days before the performance, it looks as if her recital plans, and her relationship with Joshua are hitting sour notes. Will she be able to restore harmony in time to save her musical reputation?

Butterfly Come Home—Caledonia Chronicles—Part 2 in the series of Great Lakes Romances® (Set in Caledonia and Calumet, Michigan, 1905-06.) Deborah Dapprich's flighty ways had earned her the nickname, "Butterfly," in childhood. Now, as a young woman of eighteen in the year 1905, her impetuous wanderings brought unanticipated trouble. A marriage of convenience to her childhood friend seemed the only way out. Tommy Rockwell knew that life with his Butterfly would never be dull, but he wasn't prepared for the challenges of his new bride. From Caledonia to Calumet he pursued her, only to discover that he was running second to her first love, the theater. Would she ever light long enough for his love, and the will of God, to work their way into her heart?

Fayette—A Time to Love, Eighth in the series of Great Lakes Romances® (Set in Fayette, Michigan, 1868.) The new iron-smelting town of Fayette, Michigan held no promise for sixteen-year-old Lavinia McAdams. The moment she arrived, she took an instant disliking to its muddy streets, acrid smoke, and dirty furnace men. The sooner she could return to her hometown in Canada, the better. Then Huck Harrigan came along to challenge her thinking and soften her iron will. Could she really find happiness in this raw, new town with a "pig iron" Irishman from across the bay?

Fayette—A Time to Laugh, Ninth in the series of Great Lakes Romances® (Set in Fayette, Michigan in 1879.) The greatest love of Flora McAdams' life had always been her love of animals. From girlhood she had made it her mission to care for orphaned wild creatures and hurting family pets in the pig iron town of Fayette. Now, at age eighteen, she has no lack of four-footed patients needing her skill, and no time or thought of romance, until a quiet Norwegian machinist comes to town. Sven Jorgensen hoped his first encounter with the feisty Flora McAdams would be his last. Whether at the village vegetable garden or the town racetrack, he can't seem to avoid her. But time works miracles. And after witnessing her transformation of hurting, homeless canines into healthy, loving pets, his own heart is transformed as well. Can he somehow convince her that he has much more than friendship in mind for their future?

Fayette – A Time to Leave, Tenth in the series of Great Lakes Romances® (Set in Fayette, Michigan, 1885-1891.) At age fourteen, Violet Harrigan encounters dual tragedies: the death of her father, and the resulting need to move several miles north to Fayette. The situation is more than she can bear. But a true friend sticks closer than a brother. Guy Legard visits Violet faithfully. Months turn into years, and the seed of friendship blossoms into love. Then Guy disappears into the woods for several long months and Violet turns her attention to a suave and debonair newcomer, Reggie Vanderveen. Will he steal her away to a new life of excitement in Boston, or can Guy rekindle the flame of enduring love?

Bluebird of Brockport, A Novel of the Erie Canal (Set in western New York State and on the Erie Canal, 1830) Dreams of floating on the Erie Canal have flowed through Lucina Willcox's mind since childhood. Yet once her family has purchased their boat and begins their journey, they meet with one challenge after another. An encounter with a towpath rattlesnake threatens her brother's life. A thief attempts to break in and steal precious cargo. Heavy rain causes a breach and drains the canal of water. Lucina comforts herself with thoughts of Ezra Lockwood, her handsome childhood friend, and discovers a longing to be with him that she just can't ignore. Can she have a future with Ezra and still hold onto her canalling dream? Ezra Lockwood's one goal in life is to build and captain his own canal boat, but two years into the construction of his freight hauler, funds run short. With his goal temporarily stalled, and Lucina Willcox back in his life, his priorities begin to change. Can he have both his dreams — his own boat, and Lucina as his bride?

For the Love of Roses (Set in western New York State, 1984) Reeling from the loss of her parents in a tragic auto accident, Carey McIlwain resigns her teaching job to take up the reigns of the family florist business, unaware of the challenges that await her. Gavin Jack, the darkly handsome rose supplier threatens to cut off deliveries due to lack of payment. Alex Hensley, the college botanist, wants more than friendship from their casual dates. Her younger brother Todd, who is supposed to step into the business after graduating with his Master's degree, develops a disabling addiction that threatens both his and Carey's future. Can she somehow weather the storms to find security, satisfaction, and that special someone who will steal her heart?

Trail Ride by the Yadkin River (excerpted from Rosalie of Grand Traverse Bay), (Set in Winston-Salem, North Carolina, 1900) When Vanda Mae Foxe's cherished mare takes sick and dies, she leaves a huge hole in the sixteen-year-old girl's heart. Thankfully, her daddy's expansive North Carolina horse farm has plenty of room for a new favorite, and her next-door-neighbor, Willy Jo Winthrop, offers to sell Vanda Mae the perfect horse for her.

However, Willy Jo's father insists on selling the horse to an unsavory character instead. A dispute erupts, and Willy Jo gets kicked off the family farm he loves. He takes refuge with the Foxe family and his friendship with Vanda Mae prospers as they ride beside the Yadkin River. But horse trouble trails him. Can Willy Jo solve the horse problems, reconcile with his family, and win Vanda Mae's affection as well?

MORE DONNA WINTERS TITLES

Picturing Fayette Fayette Historic Townsite in the Upper Peninsula of Michigan offers visitors a step back in time to a nineteenth century company town. Here, nestled beneath a towering limestone bluff on Lake Michigan, the Jackson Iron Company operated two iron smelting furnaces. From December 25, 1867 to December 1, 1890, hot iron poured forth into casting houses, was cooled and separated into "pigs," and shipped to Ohio aboard schooners. Today, several original structures give testimony to Michigan's industrial past—from the laborers' log cabin, to the managers' salt box homes, to the "Big White House" on the bluff that was occupied by the superintendent. In the center of all these stands the working core of the once-thriving village—the furnace stacks, casting houses, company store, warehouse, town hall, company office, machine shop, and hotel. Through the pages of this book, tour this fascinating open air museum that offers million-dollar views of the harbor, bay, and quaint remnants from nearly 150 years ago. Quotes from newspapers of that era serve as captions, bringing the town to life. Fayette Historic Townsite is without a doubt one of the best-preserved company towns in America and a gem of Michigan history that is unlike any other.

Adventures with Vinnie Handsome. Affectionate. In need of a forever home. And we were in need of another rescue dog. Thus began our Adventures with Vinnie.

From his first day to his last, the only predictable thing about Vinnie was his unpredictability. Loving and loyal, an escape artist to rival Houdini, and a genuinely comical fellow, his antics will make you laugh, give you a fright (but only for a moment), and melt your heart.

So join us, won't you? With Vinnie, there's never a dull moment!

~~~

Having retired to the Upper Peninsula of Michigan, Fred and Donna Winters decided to choose older shelter dogs for their family pets—dogs not easily placed because of their age.

When an opportunity arose in March of 2012 to add a Lab/Dobie mix to their family, they didn't hesitate. Nearly forty years of dog parenting had given them confidence that they could provide a safe, loving home for this senior pet fallen on hard times.

They hadn't anticipated the likes of Vinnie.

Learn how that loving shelter dog with bright, longing eyes, led to adventures never expected the day they welcomed him into their lives!

This book contains twelve full-color photographs of Vinnie and his family.

~~~

A Walk in the Valley—Christian encouragement for your journey through infertility by Julie Arduini, Heidi Glick, Elizabeth Maddrey, Kym McNabney, Paula Mowery, and Donna Winters

Everyone's journey through infertility is different. Even women who have the same physical problems will have different courses of treatment, different responses, and different emotional ups and downs as they walk this path. But we also have so much in common: the hurt, anger, frustration, pain, sorrow, hope and joy that we have experienced along the way. We are women who have experienced infertility. Some of us have gone on to conceive, others have adopted, and others remain childless. All of us have found peace in the loving arms of our Father God at the end of our journey. We want to share our experiences and thoughts with you. It is our hope and prayer that you'll be encouraged. This devotional workbook starts with how each woman discovered her infertility, then explores the diagnostic testing pursued, how they processed the official diagnosis, what decisions had to be explored regarding treatment, their experiences during infertility treatment (including pregnancy, miscarriage, and childbirth), and finishes with their experiences in remaining childless, adoption, foster care, child sponsorship, and the emotional healing regardless of the outcome of their infertility journey. Each devotional has a Scripture focus and questions for thought and discussion. 228 pages

Find all of Donna Winters' titles at:

www.GreatLakesRomances.com

www.ingramcontent.com/pod-product-compliance
Lightning Source LLC
Chambersburg PA
CBHW061324200626
46813CB00017B/2956